"I love the way this man writes! I adore his style. There is something about it that makes me feel as if I'm someplace I'm not supposed to be, seeing things I'm not supposed to see and that is so delicious."
REBECCA FORESTER, USA Today Bestselling Author

This book "is creative and captivating. It features bold characters, witty dialogue, exotic locations, and non-stop action. The pacing is spot-on, a solid combination of intrigue, suspense, and eroticism. A first-rate thriller, this book is damnably hard to put down. It's a tremendous read."
FOREWORD REVIEWS

"A terrifying, gripping cross between James Patterson and John Grisham. Jagger has created a truly killer thriller."
J.A. KONRATH, USA Today and Amazon Bestselling Author

"As engaging as the debut, this exciting blend of police procedural and legal thriller recalls the early works of Scott Turow and Lisa Scottoline."
LIBRARY JOURNAL

"The well-crafted storyline makes this a worthwhile read. Stuffed with gratuitous sex and over-the-top violence, this novel has a riveting plot."
KIRKUS REVIEWS

"Verdict: The pacing is relentless in this debut, a hard-boiled novel with a shocking ending. The supershort chapters will please those who enjoy a James Patterson–style page-turner"

A "clever and engrossing mystery tale involving gorgeous women, lustful men and scintillating suspense."
Foreword Magazine

"Part of what makes this thriller thrilling is that you sense there to be connections among all the various subplots; the anticipation of their coming together keeps the pages turning."
Booklist

"This is one of the best thrillers I've read yet."
New Mystery Reader Magazine

"A superb thriller and an exceptional read."
Midwest Book Review

"Verdict: This fast-paced book offers fans of commercial thrillers a twisty, action-packed thrill ride."
Library Journal

"Another masterpiece of action and suspense."
New Mystery Reader Magazine

"Fast paced and well plotted . . . While comparisons will be made with Turow, Grisham and Connelly, Jagger is a new voice on the legal/thriller scene. I recommend you check out this debut book, but be warned . . . you are not going to be able to put it down."
Crime Spree Magazine

"A chilling story well told. The pace never slows in this noir

thriller, taking readers on a stark trail of fear."
CAROLYN G. HART, N.Y. Times and USA Today Bestselling
Author

NIGHT WITNESS

Thriller Publishing Group, Inc.

NIGHT
WITNESS

R.J. JAGGER

Thriller Publishing Group, Inc.

NIGHT WITNESS

Thriller Publishing Group, Inc.
Golden, Colorado 80401

Copyright©RJJagger

ISBN 978-1-937888-92-3

For Eileen

ACKNOWLEDGEMENTS

Thanks to the many wonderful readers, booksellers, editors, publishers, agents, audio producers, book reviewers, authors, groups (including International Thriller Writers and Mystery Writers of America), proofreaders and other kind-hearted souls who amplified my efforts and who encouraged me with positive vibes over the years. Without you this book would have never happened.

1

Day One—July 12
Monday Morning

———————————

NicktTeffinger, the 34-year-old head of Denver's homicide unit, woke up in a cold sweat and realized he was in a plane. He gripped the armrests and listened for noises, the kind that meant the aircraft was two heartbeats away from a death spiral.

He heard nothing.

He listened harder, still got nothing and stretched his cramped frame before pulling two photographs out of his shirt pocket. Both were of Amanda Peterson, the victim. The first showed a 22-year-old waitress, an attractive woman with green eyes, a white smile and golden skin, with a whole life to live.

The second showed her twenty-four hours later grotesquely dead.

The man had gouged out her eyes, turned them around and reinserted them, as if she was looking at her brain.

That was a year ago.

Teffinger never caught him but he resurfaced Friday evening, thousands of miles away in the City of Light.

The plane landed uneventfully at Charles de Gaulle Airport, twenty-three kilometers north of Paris, just as the Parisian sun broke over the horizon. Normally, landings turned Teffinger into a sweaty transfixed mess. But this time he was busy running down a new theory on how to catch his killer. And, by the time the aircraft reached the terminal, he had configured a plan that might actually work.

It would be risky, insanely risky.

He had no idea if his Paris counterparts would go for it or not.

"Probably not," he muttered. "Not if they have half a brain."

He raked his thick brown hair back with his fingers. It immediately flopped back down over his forehead. When the aircraft came to a complete stop, he waited until everyone else deplaned. Then he stood up, pulled a bag out of the overhead compartment, and walked his six-foot-two frame down the aisle at his normal pace.

In the terminal, free at last, he realized something.

He needed coffee, truckloads of coffee, not in five minutes, now.

A talkative cabbie with a gold tooth named Baptiste weaved and honked his way through insane traffic and eventually dropped Teffinger off dazed but alive at the Hotel de Sille, which sat in the bustling St. Germain des Pres district in central Paris one block south of the Seine on the Left Bank. The hotel was an old narrow stone building with twenty rooms, wedged wall-to-wall between similar facades, all light gray in color but with different textures and designs. The lobby was art deco with clean lines and soft neutral colors offset by splashes of blue leather chairs and hot pink flowers.

"Ticket to Ride" came from speakers somewhere.

Teffinger liked the place immediately.

The receptionist, a curvy beauty in her early twenties, studied his eyes and said, "One's green and one's blue."

Teffinger nodded.

"One of my many flaws."

"I like your many flaws."

Her name was Sophia.

"There's a jazz club down the street called Le Cave. I'll be down there tonight, about 10:30. Maybe I'll see you there."

Teffinger nodded.

"Maybe you will."

"You should see the real Paris while you're here, the one that only the locals know."

"And you'd show it to me?"

She smiled.

"Oui."

His room was the cheapest one there—a walkup on the top floor facing the street noise. The roofline angled intrusively into the room and the bed had some kind of a cylindrical thing where the pillow should be. Teffinger didn't care, because the two necessities were there, namely a WC and a shower, as well as some peripherals such as a TV, phone and Internet access.

Good enough.

He unpacked, took a shower, and studied a map until he figured out which Metro lines he needed. Then he headed outside under a flawless Paris sky and walked past strings of crowded cafes that spilled onto the sidewalks with tables, chalkboard menus and flower arrangements. The Stone's "Ruby Tuesday" weaved out of a passing convertible and then faded away.

It was time to meet his contact, a detective.

Someone named Fallon Le Rue.

He took the Metro and decided, by the time he got off, that he wouldn't do it again, not so much because of the crowds, but because it was a waste of the five senses to be in an underground tunnel when something as spectacular as Paris sat on the surface. The artist in him had already been awakened by the charm, ambiance and mystery of the ancient architecture and the winding streets.

He needed to drink it in.

Out of the Metro and into the sunlight, he walked for six blocks and eventually found himself escorted into the office of Fallon Le Rue, who was flicking a lighter and studying papers.

She looked up.

Their eyes locked.

He sensed danger but it was too late.

His life had already changed.

2

Day One—July 12
Monday Morning

D eja Lafayette dragged her 23-year-old body out of bed Monday morning and pulled the curtain back to see what the day looked like. The familiar panorama of the picturesque Montmartre district greeted her. Sitting on a hill in northern Paris and home of the Moulin Rouge, the area had long been associated with exotica, artists, beautiful squares, winding streets and long stairways. Although tourists had rediscovered the area in recent years, there were still plenty of reasonable apartments to be had, like hers, a second-floor walkup on Rue du Mont.

The sky was flawless.

Good.

She could leave the umbrella home.

She showered, slipped her well-endowed five-foot-four body into a professional beige pantsuit, picked up her purse and took one last look in the mirror before heading out into the world. An attractive face with hypnotic hazel eyes and thick brown hair stared back—seriously sexy, although that wasn't her goal. She blew herself a kiss, headed outside and grabbed a cup of coffee and a fresh croissant from the corner café on her way to the Metro. A half hour later she emerged at La Defense, a modern business district west of Paris, filled with contemporary towers and home to more than a few of the world's most powerful corporations and law firms.

She headed for the ultra-chic EDF tower, which busted into the sky with sensuous curves and clean glass lines. Inside, she took the elevator to the thirtieth floor, which was the lowest of the three floors that housed Bertrand, Roux & Blanc, Ltd., France's largest law firm.

Yves Petit, the head of the firm's international department, discovered her last year.

At the time, she was working as a waitress at the WAGG Bar. Petit flirted with her and learned that she spoke flawless English, Italian, German and Portuguese, in addition to French. More importantly, she also wrote perfectly in all those languages, with absolutely correct grammar, punctuation and style. Even more importantly, she had a way with people.

She was just what he needed and he made her an offer.

Her job, if she wanted it, was to sit in on negotiations and meetings that involved foreign companies or affairs. She would act as an interpreter or clarifier when needed. Also, when a foreign contract or technical document needed to be drafted, the assigned attorney would take the initial stab at it to ensure that all the legal aspects were there. Deja would then clean it up and make it perfect, not only from a grammatical point of view, but also to ensure that the end product was clear and unambiguous enough to be enforced in a court of law.

When Deja walked into the lobby, the receptionist—a nonstop

flower named Natalie—said, "Hello, darling. Yves is looking for you." Deja checked her watch to be sure she wasn't late. Then she headed down a spacious art-lined corridor to Yve's office.

He was on the phone but motioned her in.

She walked to the windows and looked down.

The district buzzed, consistent with the fact that over a hundred thousand people worked there. Below, in the square, Alexander Calder's bright-red abstract sculpture looked like a five-story spider walking between towers.

Yves was 42, attractive, and a serial womanizer—but in a nice way—with brown hair that he combed straight back. As far as power in the firm of over two hundred attorneys went, he was equaled by a handful but surpassed by none. Everyone liked him, even people who shouldn't.

He hung up, looked at her apologetically and said, "I've been a bad boy."

Deja raised an eyebrow.

"How so?"

"I've taken the liberty of making a few phone calls."

She didn't understand.

"What kind of phone calls?"

"Well, the main one was to Jacques Lacan. Do you know who he is?"

"No."

"Jacques Lacan is the president of the law school, over at the university, as well as a personal friend of mine," Yves said. "I made an inquiry as to whether the school would accept you, if you were to apply. I also gave you my highest recommendation." He paused and smiled. "He had the admissions department round up your undergraduate transcripts and that kind of thing. Last night, he called me at home. Want to know what he said?"

Deja tried to say, "Oui," but her mouth wouldn't move so she just nodded.

Yves smiled, took a deliberately slow sip of coffee and said, "He said it would be their honor. Here's the way I see things unfolding, if you're interested. We're going to keep your salary at the same level here at the firm but cut your hours down to part-time. We're going to pay all your law school expenses—tuition, books, everything. Then, when you graduate, we'll bring you onboard as a fulltime attorney." He paused. "That is, like I said, if that kind of thing interests you."

She didn't know what to say and said it.

"I don't know what to say."

"Then just say, Fine, Yves, can I get back to work now?"

She almost said it, but instead hugged him, fought back tears and said, "No one's ever done anything like this before."

He smiled.

"As much as I'd like to take credit for being a nice guy, our motives are purely selfish," he said. "We want to be sure you're around here for the long haul. It's going to be interesting to watch you grow. If my hunch is right, you're going to end up being one of those attorneys who leaves their mark for a hundred years."

3

Day One—July 12
Monday Morning

Nicholas Ringer's 72-foot yacht, Le Femme Nauti, was slipped in the best place in the world, namely Nice, France. Every earthly pleasure—and every corresponding sin, for that matter—was right there within walking distance.

Food.

Gambling.

Nightlife.

Eye candy.

At six-four, age 36, with long black hair, a GQ face and a muscular sunned body, he was well equipped to take full advantage of everything this corner of the world had to offer. He owned an expansive gated villa, carved into the hill and overlooking the aqua waters of the Mediterranean, but he hardly slept there in the summer, preferring instead the lapping of the water against the hull.

He came topside to find Nodja Lefebvre heading to shore in one of the dinghies, with her long hair and a white sundress blowing in the breeze.

A note by the coffee maker said, *Groceries*.

He poured a cup of caffeine and watched her through binoculars.

She had a taut, dancer's body.

Her face was nice enough but in a subtle, easily-overlookable way. When people met her for the first time, they hardly noticed her. Then she grew on them, like an acquired taste. Ringer, however, saw something he liked right away.

He picked her up last year n a dive Paris bar while he was dressed down, looking like a cab driver who hadn't had a fare in a month. He spotted her across the room, immediately walked over and leaned in.

"I'd like to have a drink with you," he said.

She looked up.

Their eyes met.

"Here's the thing, though," he said. "I'm sort of short on cash, so you'd have to buy."

She bought him a drink.

And another.

And another.

Later that night, they made passionate, sweaty, rock star love under the stars in a dark grassy enclave next to the Seine. Ringer played the pauper for a full month, to be absolutely positive that she loved him for him and had no idea who he really was, before saying one day, "Do you feel like taking a little field trip?"

She shrugged.

"Sure, to where?"

"To a place I want to show you," he said.

He made a phone call.

Ten minutes later, a driver picked them up in a limo and whisked them to the Charles de Gaulle Airport. Ringer took the controls of his Grob Aerospace SP jet and let her ride shotgun over the Alps and into Nice.

That was last year. Now, this morning, when she got back to the *Nauti*, Ringer told her he'd be back sometime later today, got in his jet and pointed the front end north towards Paris.

He owned Ringer Shipyards, Ltd., which specialized in the manufacture of custom vessels in the 30 to 70 meter range. The facilities were located in southern Italy, not Nice—far enough away to not be a daily bother, but close enough to fly to twice a week.

Ringer vessels were world-renowned not only for their seaworthiness and state-of-the-art power plants and electronics, but also for their decadence and contemporary lines.

Each one was unique; in exterior profile; in interior layout; in furnishings.

The waiting list was a year and that was just to have a vessel started. Completion typically took another two years but the wait was worth it. At the end, the customer owned a Ringer Yacht custom-made to his or her every specification.

Shortly before noon, Ringer touched down at the Charles de Gaulle Airport, took a cab to La Defense district, and headed to the offices of Bertrand, Roux & Blanc, Ltd. Two heartbeats later, Yves Petit walked into the lobby, hugged him and said, "Good to see you again."

"Likewise. Is the other party here?"

Yves nodded.

"We're set up down the hall."

Suddenly a young woman joined them, a well-endowed

woman in a beige pantsuit, very attractive. "This is Deja," Yves said. "She'll be doing the interpreting this morning."

Ringer shook the woman's hand and liked her immediately.

They headed down a spacious corridor past pricey art, to a glass-walled conference room with a commanding view of Paris. Three Portuguese men sitting at a table stood up to shake hands when they walked in.

Ringer knew which one the buyer was right away.

He had that look to him, that unmistakable look of power and money and ego.

Three hours later, Ringer had a duly executed cost-plus contract in hand for the construction of a 65-meter Ringer Yacht. He also had a certified check in the amount of 2,000,000 euros in hand, the first partial payment.

The young woman handed Ringer a business card in the lobby, just as he pushed the button for the elevator. He took a quick look—Deja Lafayette—and raised an eyebrow.

"Lafayette. No relation to the infamous archeologist, I assume."

"Are you talking about Remy Lafayette?"

Ringer cocked his head.

"In fact, I am."

"He's my uncle," the woman said. "Do you know him?"

Ringer shrugged.

"Sort of, I took one of his classes at the university when I was picking up my business degree. That was—what?—twelve years ago, now," he said. "He gave me the lowest grade I ever had—a C+. I'm still a little pissed at him about that. How's he doing?"

The woman's face contorted.

"He's dead."

"Dead?"

She nodded and gave him the details. Remy Lafayette had been attacked in his home Monday evening, exactly one week ago. The house had been ransacked and the police were treating it as a homicide. So far, however, they had no leads, at least none that she knew about.

Ringer frowned and handed his business card to her.

"Remy Lafayette was a good man," he said. "If the police don't come up with anything, call me. I'll put the best private investigators that money can buy on the case—my treat. And don't worry about the cost. I have more money that I could ever spend." He chuckled and added, "I probably owe it to the man, in any event. If the truth be told, I only deserved a C."

The woman gripped his card and looked into his eyes.

"Thank you," she said. "We'll see what happens."

"It's a standing offer," he said. "Just say the word."

From the law firm, Ringer took a cab to CDG and then flew directly to Nice.

He couldn't get Remy Lafayette out of his mind.

He kept picturing the man dead.

4

Day One—July 12
Monday Morning

Teffinger's first thought when he saw Fallon Le Rue was that he better not fall in love with her because he'd be leaving France in a couple of days or a week. His second thought was, *Too late.* She was without a doubt one of most dangerously hypnotic women he had ever come across— taller than average; a fit body; about 27; blond hair, perfectly straight, halfway down her back; and mysterious green eyes with a raw animal lust just below the surface.

She screamed in bed, he could already tell.

She wasn't trying to be sexy. In fact, she hardly wore any makeup. Her pants and blouse were conservative. Her shoes were off. Her socks were black.

Teffinger extended his hand and said, "Nick Teffinger."

The woman set the lighter down and shook.

He liked the feel of her skin.

"Fallon Le Rue," she said. "Before we get started, it's probably best to go over a few of the preliminaries, just to be sure we're on the same page. The U.S. Marshall, Max Smith, is a good friend of this office. He vouched for you and that's why you're here. We'll share our files with you. We'll take your information and any ideas you might have. You're going to be fully in the loop. But the jurisdiction stays with us. You're strictly here in a watch-and-suggest capacity, not in a hunt-and-act capacity. We appreciate that back in the United States you're a detective and, reportedly, a very capable one. But here in France you're a civilian. Any questions?"

good friend of this office. He vouched for you and that's why you're here. We'll share our files with you. We'll take your information and any ideas you might have. You're going to be fully in the loop. But the jurisdiction stays with us. You're strictly here in a watch-and-suggest capacity, not in a hunt-and-act capacity. We appreciate that back in the United States you're a detective and, reportedly, a very capable one. But here in France you're a civilian. Any questions?"

Teffinger nodded.

"One," he said.

"Which is what?"

"Do you have any coffee?"

She smiled, and did.

Then they headed to the crime scene.

Fallon came to a stop in front of an unpretentious house on the eastern outskirts of the city, killed the engine and slipped her shoes on. Crime-scene tape circled the yard. They put on latex gloves and entered through the front door. This is where the victim had her eyes gouged out and reinserted backwards, the same as Amanda Peterson back in Denver.

Inside, Teffinger could hardly believe what he saw.

An ornate picture frame sat on a table in the corner.

Inside that frame was a color photograph, a photograph of a woman.

A woman he knew.

Tracy White.

"That's the victim," Fallon said.

"That's the victim?"

"Yes." Teffinger must have had a look on his face because Fallon added, "What's wrong?"

He shook his head in disbelief.

"I thought the victim's name was Margaux Simon."

"It is," Fallon said.

Teffinger picked up the frame and looked at it closer. "This is Tracy White."

"Tracy White? Who's Tracy White?"

Teffinger walked to the window and looked out. Then he turned and said, "This is worse than I thought."

"What do you mean?"

Teffinger slumped into a chair, leaned forward and buried his face in his hands. He didn't move for a long time. Then he looked up, locked eyes with Fallon and said, "This is my fault. This woman is dead because of me."

Fallon looked dumbfounded.

"What in the hell are you talking about?"

Teffinger needed air, not in thirty seconds, this second, so they headed outside and ended up walking down the street. He kicked a Coke can ahead.

"The dead woman in Denver, Amanda Peterson, lived on the seventh floor of a fairly large apartment building," he said. "A woman named Tracy White lived on the third floor. The building had an elevator, but Tracy was one of those health nuts who always took the stairs. On the evening when Amanda Peterson got her eyes gouged out, Tracy was coming up the stairs carrying a bag of groceries and encountered a man coming down, fast, as in two steps at a time."

A car sped by, closer than it should have, a model Teffinger had never seen before.

Small.

In a hurry.

"Anyway, Tracy worked with a sketch artist at my request and we ended up with a pretty good composite that we showed to everyone in the building," Teffinger said. "It turned out that the guy didn't live there and hadn't been visiting anyone, so we figured he was the one we were looking for. We got his picture all over town. He looked like a caveman."

She raised an eyebrow at the word caveman and asked, "Do you still have that sketch?"

"Of course."

"Did you bring it with you?"

He nodded.

"It's one of the things I want to talk to you about."

"Good," she said.

He exhaled and kicked the can as far as he could.

He mostly missed.

It only went a couple of feet.

"Unfortunately, no one called with any leads," Teffinger said. "Then a couple of days later I got a call from a man who said he was with the Colorado Bureau of Investigation. He wanted to know the correct spelling of the name of the person who gave us the sketch—their file had two different spellings. Before I could even think, I told him. It just blurted out of my mouth. As soon as I hung up, I had a bad feeling, and called back to confirm that the call had been legit. Unfortunately it wasn't."

"Meaning it had come from the killer," Fallon said.

Teffinger nodded.

"Now he had Tracy White's name, and I was the one who gave it to him," Teffinger said. "I immediately called her and offered to get her into a witness protection program. Unfortunately, she wouldn't hear of it. So then I came up with a grand plan. I figured the man would make a move sooner or later, so I started following her around—without her knowledge—

hoping I could catch the guy in the act."

"Like she was bait," Fallon said.

No, not bait.

The word *bait* implied that Teffinger went along with it, which he didn't.

"She was more in the nature of a target, one that I was intent on protecting," he said. "Anyway, to make a long story short, the guy actually showed up a couple of nights later in the parking lot of Tracy's building. Things went badly. I ended up getting shot in the stomach. The guy got away and I never got a look at him. Tracy didn't get hurt at all, but she got so freaked out that she said she was going to go into hiding and never come out. She disappeared the next day. Even I didn't know where she went."

"Apparently, she went here," Fallon said.

Teffinger nodded.

"And took the name Margaux Simon," Fallon added.

Teffinger nodded again.

"I was pretty confident that whoever killed your victim here in Paris was the same one who killed mine in Denver since the signature thing with the eyes is so unique," Teffinger said. "But now I'm positive. Somehow he tracked Tracy White to Paris. And it's all because I was stupid and gave up her name."

Fallon said nothing.

They walked in silence.

Then Fallon said, "Let's go have a look at your sketch. Time is ticking on Michelle Berri."

Michelle Berri?

"Who's Michelle Berri?"

"Tracy White's roommate," Fallon said.

"Roommate?"

"You don't know?"

No.

Teffinger didn't.

Know what?

"She's been missing since Friday night, when Tracy got killed. Our assumption is that the guy took her."

5

Day One—July 12
Monday

———————

Monday passed and Deja hardly noticed. She was too busy picturing herself as an actual flesh-and-blood attorney and trying to get a handle on everything that meant, socially, economically, and every other way. She got home shortly after six, unlocked the door and stepped inside. What she saw she could hardly believe.

The place was totally trashed.

Drawers had been pulled out and dumped.

Every picture had been taken off the wall and slit open at the back.

Her laptop was gone.

The mattress was leaning against the wall and had been sliced open, front and back.

The carpeting had been pulled up.

Almost every food product in the kitchen had been opened and dumped into the sink.

She heard a gasp behind her and turned.

A woman stood in the doorway, an exotic woman with mysterious brown eyes, golden skin and raven-black hair.

"Are you Deja Lafayette?" the woman asked.

"Oui."

"Did this just happen?"

"Oui."

The woman grabbed her arm and said, "Hurry! Come with me while there's still time!"

"But—"

"Right now! Your life is in danger!"

Deja slammed the door shut as she ran out of the apartment but didn't stop to lock it because the mystery woman had her by the hand and was pulling her down the stairs. They hurried through the crowded streets of Montmartre, not talking, looking over their shoulders. Deja saw nothing suspicious but felt eyes on the back of her head.

Very strange.

A half hour later they got to the Seine and tried to board a Batobus just as it was casting off, except they got turned away because they didn't have passes.

So they hurried down the riverside walkway instead.

They crossed over to the Left Bank at Passerelle des Arts and found a safe looking wine bar on Rue de Verneuil in the St. Germain des Pres district.

They took a private table inside, near the back, and ordered.

They kept their eyes on the door.

Everyone who came or went looked normal.

Two minutes later a frazzled waiter set a carafe of Anjon Blanc and two glasses on their table and walked off.

Deja immediately took a strong swallow and felt everything soften as the alcohol dropped warm and tingly into her stomach.

She looked at the mystery woman, her first really good look in fact.

The woman was in her late twenties, five-nine, dark, exotic and sensuous, dressed in khaki pants, a white cotton shirt and black leather shoes. She looked feminine enough to dance the can-can at the Moulin Rouge and tough enough to hunt lions on the Serengeti.

"So who are you and what happened to my apartment?" Deja asked.

"Fair questions," the woman said. "What do you know about archeology?"

"Archeology?"

"Right."

Deja wrinkled her forehead. "Absolutely nothing. Why?"

"What do you know about the work your uncle was doing?"

"Remy?"

The woman nodded.

"Nothing, why?"

"Because that's why he's dead and why you're in danger," the woman said. Then she exhaled and said, "I'm sorry, you asked who I am and I haven't told you. My name is Alexandra Reed."

"Who tore my apartment apart?"

Alexandra took a deliberately slow sip of wine, looked into Deja's eyes and said, "I don't know but I do know what they were looking for."

"What?"

"The map," Alexandra said. "They think Remy might have given it to you for safekeeping."

"Map? What map?"

"The map to the treasure," Alexandra said. "Ancient treasure."

Deja shook her head in disbelief and took another sip of wine.

"Remy never gave me anything," she said.

Alexandra didn't look impressed.

"Maybe he did and you just don't know it." She drank the rest of her wine and set the empty glass on the table. "Drink up," she said. "We have a lot of work to do."

Deja drained what was left in her glass.

"How do you know all this stuff?"

Alexandra stood up.

"All in time," she said. "Which we're wasting."

6

Day One—July 12
Monday Night

More problems than usual erupted at Ringer Ship-yards on Monday. Several vendors still hadn't delivered overdue materials that were in the critical work path of a vessel, bringing its construction to all but a standstill. A buyer from Greece who was supposed to cure a payment default today still hadn't done so. A 50-year-old worker fell off an unguarded scaffold and broke his hip, re-igniting locker room grumbling that production was being emphasized over safety.

Nicholas Ringer's phone rang all day.

Then, after dark, he got yet another call, only this one wasn't work related.

It was from Deja Lafayette, the young woman he met this morning, the interpreter, Remy Lafayette's niece.

She sounded upset.

"Is that offer for a P.I. still good?"

It was.

Absolutely.

"I only have a few seconds to talk right now but I'll call you tomorrow with more information," she said. "Here's what's going on. Someone broke into my apartment today and tore the place apart. Then a woman mysteriously showed up out of the blue. She says her name is Alexandra Reed. She says that Remy was killed because of some ancient map. A map to treasures that are supposedly buried somewhere in Egypt."

A map?

Right.

"She says that's why my apartment was torn apart, because someone thought he might have given the map to me," she added. "We're going to Remy's house in a little bit to look for it."

The map?

Right.

The map.

"Here's the bottom line," she said. "This woman says she's working for the Egyptian government on a clandestine mission. She says that the government can't be officially involved because she might be forced to do certain things that it can't afford to be associated with."

Like what?

Kill somebody?

"I don't know, she didn't specify, but that's the impression I got—something dirty or extreme," she said. "Her mission is to get to the treasure first to be sure it gets turned over to the authorities so it can take its proper place in history. These other people are nothing more than looters. I know I'm rambling, but does any of this make sense?"

"I'm following you," Ringer said.

"She doesn't want the police involved, because she can't

have anyone snooping around who might find out about her affiliation with the government," Deja said. "To me, she seems honest, but this whole thing is just so weird that I'm not sure."

"What are you saying?" Ringer asked. "That she's really one of the looters? That the whole thing is a trick to get you to cooperate?"

"I don't know what I'm saying," Deja said. "But that seems to be the big question. Who the hell is this woman? Is she legit? Is there really such a thing as a map? And if I actually help her find it, what will happen to me after I outlive my usefulness?"

Ringer paced.

"I'm going to call a P.I. friend of mine as soon as we hang up."

7

Day One—July 12
Monday Afternoon

Teffinger had no idea how Amanda Peterson's killer tracked Tracy White to Paris. Something like that would require deep information. Was the guy with the FBI or the CIA or INTERPOL? And what had Tracy White done differently in recent days or weeks that would have suddenly disclosed her location after keeping it so well hidden for a year? Did she tell her real name to the wrong person? Did she use it on an employment application?

"I'm starved," Fallon said.

Teffinger was too.

They ended up at a sidewalk table in the Latin Quarter, on the sunny side of the street, eating sandwiches and fruit wedges. Fallon sipped red wine and looked better and better every time Teffinger put his eyes on her.

"We need to get your sketch of the caveman on the news ASAP," Fallon said.

Teffinger shrugged.

"Let's talk about it," he said.

R.J. JAGGER

Talk about it?

What was there to talk about?

"Right now, he doesn't know that we've connected him to Denver. Nor does he know that I'm in Paris," Teffinger said. "If we use the Denver sketch, he's going to know. He's already seen it in the Denver newspapers."

"So?"

"So, we have an element of surprise going for us and it would be to our advantage to keep it that way."

Fallon chewed on it but wasn't impressed.

"That sketch is the best thing we have right now," she said. "Nothing's more important than getting it out. All we need is one phone call from someone who recognizes him."

Teffinger nodded.

"I understand that," he said. "But suppose no one calls—then what?"

She shrugged.

"Then at least we tried," she said.

"That's not good enough."

"I've come up with a plan but I have to warn you upfront that it's a little intense," he said.

She raised an eyebrow.

"Go on."

"Alright," he said. "We know the caveman will go to any lengths to get rid of a witness."

Fallon nodded and said, "It's almost a good thing that we don't have one."

Teffinger cocked his head.

"Maybe we do," he said.

"What does that mean?"

"It means that maybe we make one up," he said.

"I'm not following."

"Okay, here's the way it goes," Teffinger said. "We take the Denver sketch and redraw it so it looks like something from a new witness, someone from Paris. We keep the caveman's face as true to the original as possible. Then we blast it all over the newspapers and the televisions, like you want. That way we get the full benefit of the Denver sketch without tipping our hand."

Fallon smiled.

"You're more devious than I realized," she said.

Teffinger nodded.

"There's more," he said. "If no one calls in, we go to the next phase of the plan, which is this. We now have the caveman thinking there's a witness. We set someone up to play the part of that witness—someone from your department, maybe. We leak the person's name. The caveman will eventually close in, just like he did with Tracy White. What he doesn't know is that we'll be waiting for him."

Teffinger expected Fallon to react one way or the other, but instead she just chewed her food and looked at the people walking past.

After a few moments, she said, "You already tried something like that once, with Tracy White. You got shot and she almost ended up dead. So you don't exactly have a good track record of saving someone when Mr. Caveman closes in."

Teffinger frowned.

"This time will be different," he said.

"Whoever plays the part of the witness will be at an extreme risk," she said. "No matter how many people we surround him or her with."

True.

"I can't ask anyone to put themselves in that type of danger," she said.

"But—"

"Not to mention that the higher-ups in my department wouldn't allow such a thing in a million years. It runs against every policy we have."

Teffinger took a long drink of water.

Oh, well.

He was afraid of that.

"So, if it gets to that point, I'll be the witness," Fallon said. "I'll be the bait. But we'll have to do it on the side, meaning that no one else can know."

8

Day One—July 12
Monday Night

———————————

Monday night after dark, under a moonless French sky, Deja and Alexandra snuck past the crime-scene tape around Remy Lafayette's pitch-black house, broke a windowpane in the rear door, and stepped inside. They stood quietly, listening, but didn't hear anything except the sound of air moving in and out of their lungs. One step at a time, they felt their way through the dark interior and closed the window coverings, every one of them.

Then Alexandra turned on her flashlight.

Deja wasn't prepared for what she saw.

The place had been torn apart even worse than her apartment.

"This confirms it," Alexandra said. "They killed him. They were after the map. But they didn't get it. It's still here somewhere, I can feel it."

They had already wondered what the map might look like.

Alexandra didn't really know.

"It might not even be a map in the traditional sense," she said. "It might be more in the nature of an assortment of information from various sources that tells the location."

"The location to what, exactly?"

Alexandra frowned.

"Let's just leave it at ancient artifacts and treasures, for the time being," she said. "I'll explain more later."

"Why not now?"

"Because right now I'm not sure how aggressively the looters are going to pursue you," Alexandra said. "If they manage to capture you, the best thing you'll have going is to not know much."

"Capture me?"

Alexandra put her arm around Deja's shoulders and squeezed.

"I'm sorry you're in the middle of this, I really am," she said. "The best way for us to get you out of it is to find the treasure. At that point, everything becomes moot, including you."

"This can't be real," Deja said.

"Come on, let's get busy," Alexandra said. "If you were your uncle and wanted to hide something, where would it be?" Deja thought about it. She and Remy had been close. And even though she'd never shared his passion for archeology, she'd listen for hours, spellbound, when he told her about his latest trip to some desolate nook and cranny of the world. There he bought rare artifacts and priceless pieces of history from underground markets and shady traders, dangerous men who didn't ask questions and didn't expect any in return.

Everything Remy purchased, he bestowed to museums; every single thing, even things that he managed to buy for a hundredth of their value, things that could have let him retire right now in luxury.

His last trip had been to Cairo. Deja didn't know what had drawn him there, but did know that she'd rarely seen him that excited. She looked at Alexandra and said, "Remy roamed the world and bought stuff that he gave to museums."

Alexandra nodded.

She already knew that.

"But whenever he got a new piece, he would keep it around for a while," Deja added. "He had a special place where he kept them." She frowned. "Every time he showed me something, though, he already had it out by the time I got here. I never saw where he got them from."

They searched and found nothing. They searched some more and found more nothing, piles and piles of nothing.

Remy's computers were gone.

His research notes and files were gone.

His desk drawers were empty.

An hour into it, Deja excused herself to use the facilities. When she came out Alexandra was in the hallway and said, "By the way, you haven't told anyone about me, have you?"

"No, you said not to."

Alexandra wrinkled her forehead.

"I know," she said. "I just want to be sure you know how important that is. Not just to keep the government out of it, but also for me, personally. If I have to kill somebody, I don't want to end up in jail."

"You would kill somebody?"

"No," Alexandra said. "Only if they forced me and there was no other option." Deja must have had a look on her face because Alexandra added, "Make no mistake, these people are vicious, terribly vicious. They already killed your uncle."

9

Day One—July 12
Monday Night

———————

Marcel Durand loved the night. When the sun went down, the good people went to sleep and the dangerous people came out. Animal instincts got crisper and more intense.

Passion intensified.

Edges got edgier.

Women got looser.

Things happened that shouldn't, all simply because the earth rotated to the other side for a few short hours.

Sometimes, he thought that it was his love for darkness that made him such a good private investigator. But, when he thought deeper about it, he knew otherwise. It was really his desire to be where he shouldn't.

To see what he shouldn't.

To know what he shouldn't.

To do what he shouldn't.

He was only five-eleven, shorter than he wanted to be, but made up for it by staying lean and strong. His face was neither attractive nor repulsive. It was instantly forgettable. In his younger days, he viewed it as a curse. Now at age thirty he realized just how wrong he had been.

He spoke well, and not just French, English and Spanish too.

He could have easily learned other languages, but instead he concentrated on fine-tuning those two to perfection, to the point where he not only spoke them flawlessly and properly, but did so without the slightest trace of an accent. People from London took him for an American. People from Madrid took him for someone down the street.

He was the best P.I. that Paris had ever seen, or ever would.

He wasn't in the phone book; strictly word-of-mouth.

Only clients with the deepest pockets were accepted.

Tonight was nice and dark, perfect for working. Except tonight he wasn't working. Tonight he was going to feed the fetish.

It had been a long time, too long, which wasn't healthy.

He got in the car and headed to a bar called De Luna.

On the way, his phone rang and a familiar voice came through, the voice of Nicholas Ringer, who routinely used Durand to investigate buyers who wanted to have a yacht built, to be sure they weren't shady and had the capital to back up their words.

"Another potential sale in the works?" Durand asked.

"No, this is something different," Ringer said. "A lot different."

Durand took the information as he drove, jotting down notes on a pad while he steered with his knees. Then he said, "You weren't kidding when you said this was different. I'll start on it first thing in the morning."

"Thanks," Ringer said. "I'll wire a retainer to your account."

10

Day One—July 12
Monday Night

———————

When a tired-looking man named Benoit walked into Fallon Le Rue's office Monday evening and set his re-draw of the Denver caveman on her desk, Teffinger and Fallon looked at it and smiled.

"Is that what you wanted?" Benoit asked.

It was.

It was indeed.

Although the texture, attitude and feeling of the drawing had totally changed, the new face unquestionably depicted the same Neanderthal as the old one.

"We'll turn it over to the Louvre when we're done with it," Teffinger said.

Benoit grinned.

"You do that," he said. "And tell them I'll rework Mona if they want. That girl needs a smile in the worst way."

Teffinger laughed and slapped Benoit on the back.

They scanned the sketch, emailed it to every TV station and

newspaper in town, and then followed up with telephone calls. By the time the dust cleared, they had it primed to hit Paris big time starting tomorrow morning. With any luck, by noon someone would call in and tell them who the caveman was.

The sun was setting and the lights of Paris began to twinkle.

Teffinger's stomach growled.

"I heard that," Fallon said.

"Sorry."

"Hungry?"

"Starved."

"How would you like a home-cooked meal?"

"Really?"

Yes.

Really.

Fallon le Rue, it turned out, lived in a 25-meter boat docked on the Left Bank of the Seine, across from Ile St. Louis in the Latin Quarter, not more than a twenty minute walk from Teffinger's hotel. The steel-hulled vessel was clearly old but had been beautifully converted into first-class accommodations.

Very cool.

The lower level, which ran the length of the boat, was living quarters fitted with large square windows. Above that, a large outdoor sitting area occupied the rear third of the boat, encircled in a perimeter of large white planters. Vegetation six or eight foot high on the port side provided good privacy from the adjacent walkway.

On the starboard side were flowers, sitting low, not obstructing the stunning views of the river, St. Louis and Notre Dame.

The middle third of the boat was a second level of living quarters, well-encased in oversized rectangular windows, with a curved white roof and teakwood exterior.

The bow contained lockable storage spaces.

Inside, the floors and walls were warm beech and the lines were clean. All interior remnants of the vessel's rough, sea-faring workdays were gone. Now there were wall sockets, recessed lights, a modern kitchen, washer and dryer, and cable.

Teffinger must have had a look on his face because Fallon said, "I don't get paid this much. It's inheritance. What are you in the mood for, to eat?"

He shrugged.

"How about a cheeseburger and Bud Light?"

She laughed.

"You're too American, we need to French you up." Then she headed into the lower level and said over her shoulder, "I'll be right back." He took a seat on the couch. Fallon returned three heartbeats later dressed in white shorts, a black tank top and lots of skin, barefoot.

Her body was firm, strong and sensuous.

Teffinger swallowed.

He had never seen such a beautiful woman.

Well, that wasn't true.

He had.

But he had never wanted a woman so much.

That much was true.

A tattoo emerged from under Fallon's shorts and wrapped around her left leg. Teffinger studied it, then looked into her eyes and said, "I don't know what it is, but I like it."

"You want to see the whole thing?"

He raised an eyebrow.

Sure.

She closed the window coverings, dimmed the lights, poured

two glasses of white wine and handed one to Teffinger. He took a long swallow and felt it go straight to his head.

So nice.

Fallon stood in front of him and said, "I can't believe I'm doing this." Then she wiggled out of her shorts, let them drop to the floor, and stepped out. She wore a black thong, the most incredibly sexy thing Teffinger had seen in his life. She pulled the tank over her head and threw it on the couch next to him, revealing ample breasts cupped in a flimsy black bra.

The tattoo turned out to be a vine of erotic, sensuous flowers.

It covered most of her stomach, with large, prominent pedals.

Then it wrapped around her hip, down one cheek of her ass, and around her upper thigh twice, ending about six inches above her knee.

She turned around.

So he could see the back better.

If Teffinger had described the tattoo to someone, it probably would have sounded weird. But it was the coolest thing he had ever seen, expertly done, with breathtaking colors that vibrated against her skin.

He ran his fingers over it, starting on her stomach, winding around all the way to the end.

She didn't stop him and instead, unclasped her bra and dropped it to the floor.

Teffinger pulled her thong down.

Then he kissed her.

"No, not here." She grabbed his hand, led him outside to the sitting area and laid down on a cushion next to the planters. She stretched her arms above her head and wiggled her stomach.

11

Day One—July 12
Monday Night

———————

If the map was at Remy's house, Deja and Alexandra didn't find it. At first, they considered getting a hotel room for the night. Then Alexandra said, "My place is probably still safe for a day or two. I doubt that they know I'm involved yet."

She had a nice apartment in the Jardin des Plantes Quarter, on the east side of the city, fourth-floor walkup.

Everything was intact and exactly as Alexandra had left it. They ended up on the terrace with glasses of white wine, watching the City of Light twinkle.

After two glasses, Alexandra was willing to share some of her background.

She was born to French parents living in Cairo and was raised as a free-spirited female atheist in a Muslim country, which wasn't easy. She stayed there until age twenty-five, when she lost her parents to a driver who was a lot more interested in putting his wife in her place than he was in watching the road. Two months later Alexandra moved to Paris, which was the only city she knew outside Egypt.

Her parents had been archeologists.

She was too and had been for as long as she could remember.

"It started with hieroglyphics, which had a hold on me since the first time I laid eyes on them," she said. "I got fascinated with the idea of creating history by uncovering history, which sounds like a weird concept, but really isn't when you think about it. I got into it, fast and deep. The Egyptian government, which already worked with my parents, took notice and started to fund my projects. They got their money back in spades. Then they approached me about going deeper, on special assignments, ones they couldn't officially be affiliated with. The one you and I are on now is one of those underground ones. Depending on how it turns out, it may well be the most significant archeological discovery of the last thousand years."

Deja took a sip of wine.

"I'm not on it," she said. "Only you are."

Alexandra didn't look impressed but said, "Let's hope you're right."

Someone knocked on the door, someone Alexandra apparently knew and expected; a man, a shadowy man. Alexandra spoke to him in whispers while Deja waited on the terrace. Three minutes later, the man pulled his collar up, hunched his face into his shirt and left. Alexandra walked back out into the night and sat down. She showed Deja a gun and said, "Now we're not so naked." Deja wasn't sure if the sight brought relief or dread.

"That's a gun," she said.

"Do you know how to use it?"

Deja laughed at the absurdity of the question.

"No."

"This is the safety," Alexandra said. "You flick it like this to get it off. Then you're good to go."

Deja rolled her eyes but memorized the move.

Then she took a long swallow of wine.

"I work in a law firm," she said. "They're going to send me to law school this fall, all expenses paid. Being affiliated with a gun could doom me. It's the absolute last thing I need in my life right now."

Alexandra understood.

But she said, "Your job is a mere luxury, a luxury that won't keep you alive. Only you can keep you alive. Like it or not, you live in ancient times now. And in ancient times, it actually was true that only the strongest survived."

She set the gun in Deja's lap.

"I'll be right back."

She walked inside, returned with the wine bottle, and topped off their glasses. She didn't take the gun back and Deja didn't ask her to. Instead, she let it sit there, feeling its weight.

Only the strongest survived.

Remy was dead.

If he hadn't been strong enough to survive, how could Deja?

She drank more wine and fell asleep with the gun on her lap.

At some point later, which could have been ten minutes or three hours, she woke to a terrible noise coming from inside the apartment.

She was still on the terrace.

Alone.

Alexandra was no longer there.

The air was chilly.

She stood up.

The gun dropped to the floor.

She picked it up and flicked the safety off as she ran inside.

12

Day One—July 12
Monday Night

De Luna was a large bar in a basement hideaway in the Latin Quarter, a fifteen-minute walk south of the Seine. Marcel Durand didn't care about it except six times a year, namely on the second Monday of every other month, when it turned into a fetish bar. He got there just before midnight, paid 25 euros at the door, and stepped inside with a beating heart.

The place was dim and already packed.

Leather, skin, chains and masks were everywhere.

Liquor and sex permeated the air.

Several women were already on bondage display at the makeshift stages against the walls. A busty brunette wearing only a white thong, a thin bra and a mask was secured tightly and inescapable to an X-Frame. Another woman was stretched out on a rack. Another was face down on a table, hogtied and gagged. Another was in a standing position, with her wrists tied together and stretched high above her head. And there were five or six more.

Durand's cock tightened.

He ordered a double Jack, downed it and ordered another.

Flat-panel TVs throughout the club played bondage movies.

Lots of females milled in the crowd. In fact, there were probably more women than men, women of all flavors.

Hardcore.

Curious.

Exhibitionists.

Teasers.

But a good number of them were prostitutes, trolling for the big money, willing to get kinky but only for the right customer and the right price. Those were the women Durand was most interested in.

But there was no need to rush.

He had all night.

He wandered over to take a closer look at the woman stretched out on the rack, who was attracting a crowd.

The rules were simple.

Admire but don't touch, unless the guy standing guard gave the okay. Sometimes the guy was a boyfriend and didn't allow any touching at all. Other times, the guy was a pimp and allowed touching for a price. Even then, though, no sexual or inappropriate contact was permitted.

The girl on the rack must have been a whore, because the man by her was accepting money and letting people, one at a time, feel her.

Durand watched, mesmerized, and figured out the exchange rate; five Euros for sixty seconds.

No meanness or pain was allowed, only caressing, and not the crotch or the tits.

A female was now doing the feeling. She ran her hands down her captive's arms. When she got to the woman's armpits, she detected a reaction.

"Are you ticklish?" she said.

"No."

"Good, then you don't mind if I do this."

She wiggled her fingers in the woman's underarms. At first, the woman bit her lower lip and didn't respond. Then she busted out in laughter. The next person up, a man, spent his entire minute tickling her.

So did the one after that.

Then the woman had enough and asked to be released.

No problem, though. Another woman with long blond hair, wearing a white mask, came over to take her place. She spoke briefly to the man taking the money and then, right there next to the rack, she stripped off her street clothes until she got down to a black thong and matching bra.

Durand watched.

She had quite the body, quite the body indeed, plus some kind of large tattoo on her stomach.

Good.

A wild woman.

She laid down on the rack, raised her arms above her head and stared at the ceiling.

The crowd clapped.

Two men cuffed her, stretched her tight and then wrapped a blindfold over her eyes, on top of the mask. Durand wedged in closer to take a better look at the tattoo.

It was a vine of exotic, sensuous flowers.

It started on the woman's stomach and wrapped around her hip, over her ass and then twice around her upper thigh, ending about six inches above her knee.

A man paid 5 euros and immediately went to work directly on the woman's armpits. The crowd watched, hypnotized, wondering if she was another ticklish one.

She was, even more so.

Durand laid down 5 Euros and waited for his turn.

13

Day Two—July 13
Tuesday Morning

———————

Teffinger woke before dawn on Tuesday morning. The lights of Paris bounced off the Seine and bathed Fallon's sleeping body in a warm patina. Teffinger studied the sensuous curves of her naked body as he dressed and pitied every guy in the world who wasn't him. He kissed her imperceptibly before he left, walked to his hotel, and jogged five kilometers on the banks of the river as the city woke up.

Recharged.

That's how he felt.

He showered and came downstairs to find the curvy beauty from yesterday, Sophia, behind the reception desk. "You never came to the club last night," she said.

True.

He got busy.

"Too bad," she said. "You missed out."

"On what?"

She ran a finger down his chest and said, "On everything. I knocked on your door last night. You didn't answer. I may never forgive you."

Really?

Yes, really.

He pulled a rose out of a vase, pinched off the stem, and worked it into her lapel. "There, pretty in pink—forgive me now?"

She did—

—But only if he promised to take her out for a drink at some point, if not tonight, then soon.

He shrugged.

"Sure."

"No, not sure, sure means nothing. You need to promise," she said.

Fine.

He promised.

She smiled and kissed him on the cheek.

"Don't break your promise, Nick Teffinger from America. Otherwise I won't show you my tattoo."

He raised an eyebrow.

"You have a tattoo?"

She looked around, saw no one, unbuttoned her shirt and pulled up her bra. Her breasts were perky and perfect. On the left one was a tattoo.

A pink rose.

Teffinger couldn't believe it.

"It's almost a perfect match," he said, referring to the one he just put in her lapel.

She nodded.

"That's why I had to show you." Then she took his hand and put it on. "Smooth, isn't it?"

When Teffinger got to Fallon's office, she wasn't there yet, so he sat at her desk and spent half his time studying the Tracy White file and the other half ping-ponging between the coffee machine and the restroom. He didn't read French, but did understand the steps of the investigation and the forensic reports.

Fallon had done a good job.

Teffinger wouldn't have done anything differently.

Unfortunately, there were no forensic leads or witnesses.

The file had photographs and information on Michelle Berri, the missing roommate who hadn't been seen or heard from since Friday evening when Tracy White got murdered. She was five-three, 24, blue eyes, brown hair, mildly but not wildly attractive, and worked in the preservation department at the Louvre. Most likely, she was already home, or unexpectedly came home, while Tracy White was getting her eyes gouged out. Her blood hadn't been found at the scene. Nor was there any other evidence to suggest that she had been killed there. What Teffinger couldn't figure out is why the caveman didn't just slit her throat then and there.

That's what he would have done.

Why go to the bother and risk of keeping her alive and dragging her out into the world?

When Fallon showed up, Teffinger looked up and said, "Motive, that's what we need to figure out to get Michelle Berri back. What was the caveman's motive to take her instead of slitting her throat right then and there?"

Fallon grunted.

"Here's the problem," she said. "You have two pots of coffee in your gut and I don't."

She tossed a newspaper on the desk, said "Page 5," and then disappeared out the door.

Page 5 was beautiful.

The sketch of the caveman was there; big and clear, with a nice story.

There was no mention of Fallon Le Rue by name, meaning that their plan to pretend that she was the witness behind the sketch hadn't been spoiled.

Teffinger expected Fallon to be back in thirty seconds, holding a cup of coffee. Instead, she didn't return for ten minutes. When she did, she had coffee in one hand and two pieces of paper in the other.

"The caveman calls are already coming in," she said, "two potential suspects so far, both different guys. Let's go."

Teffinger fell into step and followed her out the door.

"Hold it," he said.

He ran back into the office and returned three heartbeats later with his cup in hand.

"Okay," he said.

Fallon rolled her eyes, turned and walked down the hall.

Teffinger made sure they were alone and said, "I woke up last night. You weren't there."

"Sometimes I have trouble sleeping," she said.

"Where were you?"

"I took a walk," she said. "It's what I do. Let's go." A pause, then, "We need to figure out how we're going to do this. We can't let these guys see you, because you're supposed to be in Denver. And we can't let them see me, because I might have to end up being the witness-slash-bait, which won't work if they know I'm the detective."

Teffinger thought about it and said, "I have a plan."

Fallon look surprised.

"You do?"

Yes.

He did.

"What is it?"

"My plan is to come up with a good idea as soon as possible."

Fallon chuckled and punched him in the arm.

"I don't know if I can take a whole day of you," she said.

"Few can," he said. "In fact, the only one I know of is Sydney Heatherwood."

"Who's she?"

"A detective I work with," he said.

Fallon must have detected something in his voice because she gave him a sideways look and asked, "Are you sleeping with her?"

"No. She doesn't have time. She's too busy reprogramming my truck radio to hip-hop stations."

"Did you ever?"

"What?"

"Sleep with her."

Teffinger chuckled and said, "No, even I have a few boundaries. I bounced a quarter off her ass once, but that's a whole separate story."

They took her car and pointed the front end west, still not sure how they were going to handle things when they got to where they were going.

14

Day Two—July 13
Tuesday Morning

The terrible noise last night was a man beating the life out of Alexandra Reed. Deja fired the gun before she even knew what she was doing. The man stumbled backwards, grabbed his upper chest, gurgled something painful, and hobbled out the door. They immediately slammed it shut, locked it and pointed the gun at it. When nothing happened, they went to the terrace and looked down.

A shadowy figure stumbled out of the building.

Hurt badly.

A car squealed up the street and skidded to a stop. The back door opened, a strong arm pulled the man inside, and the driver floored it while the door was still open. The acceleration slammed it shut and then the taillights disappeared around the corner.

Deja set the gun on the kitchen table and held her hands together to keep them from shaking.

"If he dies, I just killed a man," she said.

Alexandra said, "Screw him," and hugged her.

Tight and long.

They listened for the sounds of neighbors coming.

No one came.

Not a single person knocked on the door.

After a long time, they turned on the lights. Alexandra's face was a bloody mess. The man's blood was on the floor, lots of it, plus something they didn't expect—a wallet. The driver's license belonged to someone named Pascal Lambert, a 42-year-old man with a mean face.

"Do you know him?" Deja asked.

"No."

They cleaned Alexandra's face.

Then they confirmed that no one was in the hallway and quietly wiped up all the blood droppings, plus the ones in the stairway.

No doors opened while they worked.

They grabbed their purses, threw the gun in Alexandra's, and got the hell out of there.

They watched the building from the shadows across the street to see if any lights turned on or if any cops showed up. Everything stayed normal. An hour later, they walked down to the Seine, found a dark grassy enclave and fell asleep with their arms around each other.

That was last night.

Now the first light of morning softened the eastern sky. Dawn would break in a half hour. They washed their faces in the river.

Deja asked, "What do we do with the gun? Should we throw it in the water?"

Silence.

Then Alexandra said, "No, we might need it. You need to

go to work today, just as if nothing happened."

Deja agreed and they headed for her apartment.

"By the way, I don't think I told you thanks for last night," Alexandra said.

"No problem."

"He would have killed me. I could feel it in his fists."

Deja nodded.

"What I don't get is how he connected you and me together so fast."

"He must have seen us together and followed us," Alexandra said. "Maybe he tailed us to Remy's last night. Maybe he thought we found the map and that's why he came over, to get it. He probably figured we'd never tell him where it was so he'd just kill us upfront and then search the place at his leisure without having to worry about us screaming or something."

Deja nodded.

It made sense.

"I told you these guys were vicious," Alexandra added.

Deja grunted.

"I'm starting to see your point."

Mid-morning, Deja's cell phone rang at work and the voice of Nicholas Ringer from Nice came through. "I just wanted to let you know that I retained a P.I. last night, a man named Marcel Durand. He's a little edgy but he's the best there is, so we're in good hands."

"Thank you so much."

"No problem," Ringer said. "As soon as he calls me with something, I'll call you."

Deja briefly considered telling him about last night so he better understood the gravity of the situation, but decided against it.

"When is he going to start?" she asked.

"Today. I told him to make it a top priority and he promised he would."

Ten seconds after she hung up, the phone rang again. She thought it was Ringer calling back to tell her something he'd forgotten, but it turned out to be Alexandra.

"My guess is that all Remy's stolen stuff is at this guy's house, this Pascal Lambert guy. We need to get over there and get it before it disappears," she said.

"You're kidding, right?"

No.

She wasn't.

"Tonight," she added. "After dark."

15

Day Two—July 13
Tuesday

———————————

arcel Durand didn't get his P.I. posterior home until four in the morning and slept until noon to prove it. His head throbbed from too much Jack and his tongue felt like someone had taken a hairdryer to it. He popped three aspirins, drank water until his eyes floated, climbed into the shower and pissed into the drain while he lathered up.

After coffee and croissants at a café table in the sun, he started to get functional again.

There.

Better.

Time to work.

Which file should he start on first?

He chuckled.

That was easy.

The file of the client who was paying the most money.

Which meant the mystery-man file.

All he had to start with was a license plate number, the one provided by the client, but that was more than enough. It took all of two minutes to get the vehicle's registration information.

Luc Trickett.

That's who owned the mystery car.

It took another two minutes to get a printout of his driver's license. According to that, he was six-three, 235 pounds, 37-years-old and looked like a boxer.

An ugly boxer.

An ugly boxer with a crooked nose and a scar on his chin.

He turned out to live in a rundown house ten kilometers south of Paris. Durand drove past the place in the early afternoon, found all the window coverings closed, and pictured rats in the basement. No cars were in the driveway and he detected no signs of movement.

He headed back to his office to do deeper research on the man.

It wasn't pretty.

Mid-afternoon he was feeling horny, so he headed over to Verdant Park and got a 50-euro blowjob behind a tree from a blond with bloodshot eyes who said she was twenty-five but looked forty.

There.

Better.

On the way back to his office, he called the client and said, "The man's name is Luc Trickett." Then he told him everything he'd found out so far. "The guy's dangerous," he added. "What's your interest in this man, anyway?"

"It's better that you don't know."

"That may be, but my advice is to keep your distance."

Silence.

"You want me to keep digging, or is what I gave you enough?" Durand asked.

"Keep digging," the client said. "Get into his house and have a look around."

"For what?"

"I don't know," the client said. "Just get deeper information on him. Be sure you're keeping everything absolutely confidential. Not a word of this to anyone."

16

Day Two—July 13
Tuesday Morning

———————————

The first caveman call this morning was anonymous and the voice message was short: "The guy in the paper, the one on page 5 who you're looking for, looks like a DJ who plays sometimes at Rex, except it can't be him because he has a mustache and goatee and his hair is a lot longer."

"What's Rex?" Teffinger asked.

"It's one of those high-energy dance places with a thousand speakers," Fallon said.

"Have you ever been there?"

She nodded.

"Years ago."

Teffinger studied the cityscape as Fallon coped with traffic.

"Mr. DJ sounds interesting," Teffinger said. "He kills Amanda Peterson in Denver, while on vacation or business or something, and then returns to Paris. Out of an abundance of caution, he grows a moustache and a goatee and lets his hair get longer. That's exactly what I would do. Then one day, quite by accident, he sees Tracy White somewhere, maybe even at Rex. He gets enough information to find out where she lives. He's concerned that she'll spot him on the street someday, when he isn't aware of it, and make a call to the cops. So to keep that from happening, he takes her out."

Teffinger exhaled.

Then added, "In fact, that solves the issue of how he tracked Tracy White here to Paris. He didn't. They were both here the whole time and finally bumped into each other. Unfortunately for Tracy White, the caveman saw her but she didn't see him."

Fallon frowned.

"But why would he do his eyes trick? It's such a signature move, there's no upside to it. All he does is create a risk of tying himself to the Denver murder."

Teffinger shrugged.

"That's how he gets his kicks. Something inside him sounds a warning to not do it that way. But something even stronger— some recessed caveman gene—tells him to take the pleasure while the pleasure's there. After all, how many chances is he going to get?"

Fallon saw his point but added, "It could be a copycat, too."

She stepped on the brakes to avoid running over a pedestrian who suddenly darted into the street. She honked the horn, powered down the window and gave him the finger.

"Jerk!"

Then she pulled the lighter out of her purse and flicked it as she drove. Two blocks later she said, "I wonder if this guy has ever done his signature move anywhere else besides Denver and Paris. Did you ever research it?"

No.

He hadn't.

"Could be interesting," Fallon said.

Teffinger chuckled and said, "I'm confused. Are you one step ahead of me or am I one step behind?"

She grinned.

Teffinger stretched and said, "We need to find out if Tracy White has been to Rex in the last week or two or three."

"Or any of the other clubs our friend DJ'ed at," she added.

"I was going to say that next."

"It would also be nice to know if he was in the United States last year when Amanda Peterson got killed."

Right.

"I was going to say that next after the first thing I was going to say next," Teffinger said.

"How does someone even get an idea like that?" Fallon asked. "I've heard of killers gouging out eyes. But I've never heard of anyone reinserting them backwards, to make them look at their own brains. I don't get it."

Teffinger grunted.

"There are billions of people in the world. You got to expect a few weirdoes."

She gave him a sideways look.

"That's your explanation?"

He nodded.

"I'm a deep thinker," he said. "It's one of my curses."

The second call this morning was also anonymous, from a woman. "The picture on page 5, I'm not positive, but he looks an awful lot like a taxi driver who gave me a ride about six or seven weeks ago. He was driving for Les Taxis Bleus. It was at night, about one in the morning, on the Avenue des Champs–Elysees, that's where he picked me up. For some reason, the guy really gave me the creeps. That's all I can remember, sorry."

They parked outside Les Taxis Bleus, headed inside and ended up speaking to a man with a lazy eye up top and clothes that smelled like a forest fire down below.

Someone named Roland, reportedly a manager who worked there forever.

Fallon opened the paper to page 5 and tapped her finger on the sketch.

"Does this guy work here?"

Roland studied it, then shook his head.

"No, no way. That ain't no one who works here."

"You sure?"

"Let me put it this way, I know everyone who works here, and I ain't never seen this man before."

"He might have been here a couple of months ago but quit since then," Fallon said.

"Same thing," Roland said. "I don't forget no faces. Especially cavemen."

Outside, back in the car, Fallon said, "So what do you think? Is he covering up?"

"He didn't strike me as someone who gets overly hung up on helping the cops, if that's what you're getting at," Teffinger said. "But that doesn't necessarily mean he was lying in this particular instance."

Fallon rolled her eyes.

"So what you're saying is, you don't know."

"Precisely," Teffinger said. "I don't know, but with precision." He got serious and added, "It probably wouldn't hurt to talk to another supervisor or two and get a second opinion."

Fallon's cell phone rang.

She answered and listened without talking. Then she flicked it shut and said, "That was the boss man, Targaux. He wants me back at the office."

Right now.

This minute.

17

Day Two—July 13
Tuesday Afternoon

———————

Not knowing if the man died after he got whisked away in the car last night grated more and more on Deja's nerves as Tuesday wore on. She might have killed him and there was nothing she could do to undo it. True, he had it coming, and looking back on the event even in hindsight, she wouldn't have done anything differently. Except maybe shoot him in the leg instead of the chest, if she'd had the presence of mind.

Lots of questions tugged at her.

Was it legally a crime or was it self-defense?

Would she go to jail if caught?

Should she report it now, today, or keep quiet?

Was failing to report it a separate crime?

How about wiping up the blood in the hall and stairs?

Who were the people in the car? Were they hell-bent on revenge? Was the man one of their brothers? Did they know that she was the one who did it? Were they hunting her at this very moment? Were they outside the tower, waiting to grab her at the first chance?

What about the gun?

Should they dispose of it?

If so, what was the best way?

She stayed at her computer as much as she could throughout the day, avoiding face-to-face contact, especially with Yves Petit. If Deja let him look into her eyes for more than five seconds, he'd be able to tell something was wrong.

He'd probe.

She wasn't sure she'd be able to resist him.

One good thing did come out of last night. Namely, she now had a better feeling for who Alexandra Reed was, down in her core. Her concerns about Alexandra being in a conspiracy were gone.

Late afternoon, Nicholas Ringer called.

"Okay," he said, "my P.I. friend, Marcel Durand, has been able to dig up some preliminary background on Alexandra Reed." Then he gave her the information.

Alexandra was an archeologist and reportedly a very good one.

She did a lot of work for the Egyptian government.

She grew up in Egypt and moved to Paris three years ago, following a traffic accident that killed her parents.

"Do you speak Egyptian?" Ringer asked.

No.

She didn't.

Why?

"A lot of this is online, from newspaper articles and things like that," he said. "I can email the links to you if you want, except that they won't mean much if you don't read Egyptian."

"Don't bother," Deja said. "I can already tell we're pointed in the wrong direction. What I'm a lot more interested in is who killed Remy."

She paused and almost added, "Something happened last night," but she didn't.

No one should know about that until she could think it through.

And she wasn't even close.

Ten minutes later, Alexandra called. "I've been staking out Pascal Lambert's house all afternoon. There was a car in the driveway all day. I'm not positive, but I'm pretty sure it was the one from last night. It has four doors and it's the same size. Three other cars have been coming and going. There are at least six different men involved, plus two women."

Two women?

Right.

Weird.

Deja always pictured the looters as strictly male.

"I'm guessing that they haven't figured out yet that the guy's wallet is missing," Alexandra added. "Otherwise, they wouldn't be there."

Deja nodded.

That made sense.

"Do you recognize any of them?" she asked.

"I'm too far away to make out faces," Alexandra said. "At least a hundred meters, maybe more. Wait a minute, this isn't good."

What?

What wasn't good?

"Hold on," Alexandra said.

Deja stood up.

She bit her lower lip and paced.

Then Alexandra said, "Two men just carried something big out of the house and put it in the trunk of the car. I think it's our friend. I'm guessing he died and they're getting ready to dump the body."

Deja gasped and felt a presence behind her.

She turned, to find Yves Petit standing there.

"Is something wrong?" he asked.

18

Day Two—July 13
Tuesday Night

———————

Tuesday night after dark, Marcel Durand parked his P.I. ass in the shadows where he had a clear view of the house of the target, Luc Trickett, who was currently inside doing who knows what. Normally, this type of thing didn't bother him. He'd broken into lots of houses over the years without an incident. But something about the boxer made his palms sweat and his eyes dart.

Durand couldn't afford a confrontation.

The man would crush him.

Lights went on and off inside the house.

Then in quick succession they all flicked off. The boxer bounded out the front door, got in his car, slammed the door and squealed down the street. Durand stayed where he was for five minutes. Then he hugged the shadows as best he could while he inched his way towards the structure.

He put on latex gloves and tried the back door.

It was locked, so were all the windows.

He wanted to get in and out as quickly as possible, but resisted the urge to break a window and instead worked on the lock until he got it open.

He stepped inside and heard nothing other than his own breathing.

He left the door unlocked, turned on a flashlight and found he was in the kitchen. A quick look around showed nothing of interest.

The living room had a small office built into the front corner.

A laptop sat on a scratched wooden desk.

Durand booted it up, copied the files, and shut it down.

Just as he did, he heard a noise from somewhere at the back of the house.

He immediately turned off the flashlight, walked quietly to the stairs and took them, two at a time, to the upper level. He found a dark hallway, tiptoed to the end, entered a room and briefly flicked the flashlight to get oriented.

It was a bedroom.

The window overlooked the driveway.

He looked down.

Weird.

The boxer's car wasn't there.

But someone was definitely in the house.

Durand stepped behind the door and breathed as quietly as he could.

A short time later, the upstairs hallway light turned on and footsteps approached. Durand looked with one eye through the crack between the door and the jam.

The man wasn't the boxer.

Durand had never seen him before.

He wore all things black—stalking clothes—and carried a

gun.

Whoever he was, he stepped inside the room for a moment, checked in the closet and under the bed, saw no one, and walked out. He did the same to the two other rooms upstairs. Then he turned out the lights and went back downstairs.

Durand's heart raced.

He had no weapon, only fists.

Strong fists, scrappy fists, but still only fists.

From what he could tell, the man was ransacking the office. It sounded like he was emptying the desk drawers into a suitcase. Every so often, a stray bounce of flashlight punched a wall. The man walked repeatedly to the window, pulled the covering to the side and looked out.

Then the ransacking stopped.

But the man didn't leave.

Durand pictured him sitting on the couch in the dark.

Waiting.

Luc Trickett didn't show up for two full hours. And when he did, he was singing an old U-2 song with a terrible voice, slurring the words, and swearing because he couldn't get the stupid key into the stupid lock.

Drunk.

Finally he got inside.

He slammed the door shut as he headed across the living room to the kitchen.

Then, Pop!

The sound of a gun.

The air in Trickett's lungs squeezed out of his mouth and nose with a terrible noise.

A lamp crashed followed by the thud of a body hitting the floor.

Pop!

Pop!

19

Day Two—July 13
Tuesday Morning

———————

Jacques-Pierre Targaux, the head of homicide, had the eyes of a hunter and the grip of a mason. He nodded to Teffinger, gave Fallon a hug and said, "Thanks for coming in so fast." Then he introduced a man who had been seated but was now standing to shake hands, a man named Paul Sabater.

He wore a wool-blend suit.

A silk tie.

A gold watch.

He seemed vaguely familiar.

He was an attorney from the law firm of Bertrand, Roux & Blanc, Ltd.

"We're here on sort of a delicate political matter," Targaux told Fallon. "As you may or may not be aware, the law firm that Mr. Sabater is associated with represented a lot of the developers and groundbreakers for La Defense. As a result, the firm has made more than a few enemies along the way."

Fallon nodded, understanding.

She must have seen the confusion on Teffinger's face because she said, "La Defense is a business district just west of here. It's been a hotbed of controversy ever since it started going up, because it doesn't retain the historic architectural lines of Paris."

Targaux opened today's paper to page 5 and tapped his finger on the sketch. "The problem is that Mr. Sabater has somewhat of a resemblance to the person you're looking for."

Teffinger shook his head and now realized why the guy seemed familiar.

"No one has called his name in," Targaux added. "But it's only a matter of time. Mr. Sabater wants to be sure we nip this in the bud, so the firm's enemies can't use it to smear their reputation." He looked at Fallon and added, "I told him that any bud-nipping would have to come from you, since you're the person in charge of the investigation."

Sabater looked at Fallon, cleared his throat and said, "The article says that this crime happened Friday evening. Is that true?"

Fallon nodded.

"It is."

Sabater exhaled, visibly relieved.

"I was in Madrid all weekend at a law conference," Sabater said. "My wife and I, and two other couples, flew out of Paris on Thursday afternoon and didn't get back until Sunday afternoon. I was actually one of the speakers on Friday afternoon. My lecture went to approximately five o'clock. Afterwards, all six of us, and about a hundred other people, attended a dinner reception that lasted until midnight. We took a limousine back to the hotel."

He opened a leather briefcase, pulled out a pile of papers and handed them to Fallon. "It's all here," he said. "Airline tickets, hotel reservations, confirmations, cab receipts, credit card receipts with my signature, you name it." He pulled a piece of paper out of his suit coat pocket, unfolded it and handed it to her. "This is a list of the people who can verify my presence."

Fallon studied it.

Teffinger looked over her shoulder. There were six or eight names on the paper, together with titles, addresses and phone numbers. "I have to be honest with you," he said. "If you don't see the need to call them, or only one of them, that would be fine with me. I really don't want anyone to think there's smoke and therefore fire."

"I understand," Fallon said. "We'll be discrete."

"Please check it out to your total satisfaction," Sabater said. "All I'm looking for is the ability to tell reporters or anyone else who may raise an eyebrow that I wasn't involved in any way and that I voluntarily provided you with everything I had, so you could direct your investigation in a more productive direction."

"We'll check it out," Fallon said. "Just out of curiosity, who were the two other couples you and your wife were with?"

"One was Xavier and Anne Cannel," he said. "Anne is actually an attorney with one of our competitive law firms, Girard & David, Ltd. Her address and number are on the paper I just gave you. The other couple was Leroy and Monique Lacan."

Targaux leaned forward.

"Are you referring to Leroy Lacan, the judge?"

Yes.

He was.

"Leroy and I go way back," Targaux said. He looked at Fallon and said, "Why don't you let me give him a call? It'll give me a chance to see what he's been up to."

"Fine," Fallon said. Then she looked at Sabater and said, "You've gone to an awful lot of trouble to show you're not involved."

He nodded.

"I know it looks weird, but there are good reasons," he said. "First, someone will call my name in sooner or later, if they haven't already."

"No one has yet."

"Still, someone will," Sabater said. "I'd rather talk to you down here than have you show up at the firm. Second, clients operate on emotion as much as intelligence, and perception is everything. If they even think that something's amiss, there are a dozen other firms in town just as capable as ours who could handle their work. If any of them make the connection and start raising eyebrows, the firm needs to be in a position to immediately say that I've already been cleared. Third, my reputation is on the line. If the firm associates me with a loss of clients, or if some of the lawyers in the firm wonder if I might actually be involved, well, that's not a good thing for me. I've worked my entire life to get where I am. I can't afford to fall down some slippery slope just because some idiot killer looks like me."

"Understood."

After Sabater left, Targaux called Judge Lacan who unequivocally vouched for Sabater's presence in Madrid all weekend. In fact, the judge provided a web link to a video that showed the ceremonies Friday night, with Sabater clearly visible at several different times. Fallon and Teffinger checked out the rest of the story and found it solid. "Well, that was one great big waste of time," Teffinger said. "Some stupid-ass lawyer gets worried about losing billable hours and the end result is that Michelle

Berri's life gets put on hold for an extra hour. I have half a mind to call the guy up and tell him what a counterproductive selfish little twit he is."

Fallon didn't agree.

"He saved us a trip out there and had everything organized upfront," she said. "So he actually saved us time. Let's get going on the DJ."

Right.

The DJ.

20

Day Two—July 13
Tuesday Night

———————

After dark, Deja and Alexandra found deep shadows fifty meters away from Pascal Lambert's house, pulled out binoculars, and tried to make out what they could through the few slits of windows that weren't covered.

From what they could tell, there were two men inside.

Looters.

Neither of them was Pascal Lambert.

"He's dead," Deja said.

"If he is, he had it coming," Alexandra said. "And I'm not just talking about the attack on me. He's probably the one who killed Remy." A pause, then, "I think you'd be better off dropping out of this thing at this point. Go to London or something until it blows over."

Deja had already thought of that.

"I can't," she said.

Alexandra moaned.

"The only reason I contacted you in the first place was to

see if Remy gave you the map, or see if you knew where his secret hiding places were," Alexandra said. "Now that those are dead ends, there's no reason for you to be involved."

"I'm not running," Deja said.

"It's not a matter of running, it's just a matter of not having a dog in the fight anymore," Alexandra said. "Besides, I'm not so sure I'm going to give you a choice. I don't want your blood on my hands if things get ugly."

"My blood is my business," Deja said. "And besides, I do have a dog in the fight. Remy's dead and my apartment's trashed, remember?"

Alexandra frowned.

"Are you always this stubborn?"

"No, but remember what you said, namely that I won't be safe until the treasure is actually found, at which point everything becomes moot, including me. So I'm going to help you find it."

"There's nothing you can add, though."

Deja disagreed.

"You need help," she said. "This is too big for one person."

Suddenly a vehicle came up the road. It pulled into Lambert's driveway and the headlights turned off.

A woman got out, carrying a briefcase.

She knocked on the door and got let in.

Deja and Alexandra watched for a long time but nothing happened. It didn't look like the house would be left unguarded tonight, meaning they wouldn't be able to break in and get Remy's stolen papers. But they had nothing else to do and the night was warm so they sat down, stretched their legs out and waited. Neither of them recognized the woman with the briefcase, but Alexandra speculated that she was someone versed in hieroglyphics and had been brought in to interpret some of the source documents from Remy's files.

"I'm in deep enough to have the right to know more fully what's going on," Deja said.

Alexandra cocked her head, considered it and sighed.

"Okay," she said. "But this doesn't go past you. You need to promise that."

No problem.

Now talk.

"Let me give you some background," Alexandra said. "Six months ago, a tomb was discovered in the Valley of the Kings, which is in Egypt. It was the tomb of a pharaoh from the Eighteenth Dynasty, around 1375 BC, during the period of Egyptian history known as the New Kingdom. It turned out that the tomb had been robbed early on."

"How would anyone possibly know that?" Deja asked.

"Easy," Alexandra said. "A hole about a meter in diameter had been chipped into the outer doorway. Some of the chippings of the original wall were found inside on the floor. To conceal the crime, the robbers filled in the hole after they left and re-plastered the exterior. That was good enough to trick the naked eye back in that time period, but it's easily detectible by modern technology."

"Okay."

"More importantly, though, that hole only got them into one chamber. There were five chambers total, which were separated by solid walls, or what we call blockings. Holes had also been chipped into those blockings and, of course, there had been no need to reseal or re-plaster them because they couldn't be seen from the outside. So they were still in place when the tomb was discovered."

Headlights came up the road, then disappeared in the other

direction.

They didn't stop at Lambert's house.

"Okay, that might show it was robbed," Deja said. "But how would you know when it was robbed? You said it was robbed early on—"

Deja nodded.

"Lots of tombs have been robbed over time," Alexandra said. "In the early days, only the intrinsically valuable items such as jewelry from treasury caskets and precious metal vessels would be taken. All the other things such as lotions and fruits and senet games and writings and pottery and documents would be left behind because they were worthless. In the later days, however, everything would be taken, because it all now had a historical value. In this particular case, only the most valuable items had been taken, so we know it happened early on. Is this making sense?"

Yes.

Perfect.

Keep going.

"There's another thing," Alexandra said. "It was common to place jewelry and amulets and other items on the mummified body, under the wrappings. These would usually end up cemented to the body over time due to the embalming resins. Lots of mummies have been found unwrapped and then cut to pieces—literally with their arms and legs and heads detached—to get the gems off. In this particular case, however, it looked like everything had been wedged out with a knife. So we think that the robbery followed very close in time to the burial itself."

"That was gutsy," Deja said.

"Very gusty," Alexandra said. "They had totally desecrated

a member of royalty and had disrupted his travel into immortality. If they had been caught, at a minimum, they would have been beaten on the feet—known as bastinado—followed by impalement on a sharp stake."

"Ouch."

Right.

Ouch.

"Now here's the important part," Alexandra said. "Tombs usually contained inventory dockets that were scribed at the time of the funeral. This particular tomb was no exception and the list was well intact. So there is a list of everything that should have been there. Comparing the list to what was actually found tells us what was taken. The items that were stolen, to put it mildly, are staggering. Probably the most remarkable missing item is a gold mask, which according to its description, is much larger and more magnificent than the one found in the tomb of King Tutankhamun."

Who?

King Tut.

Oh.

"Anyway," Alexandra said, "none of the missing items have ever shown up anywhere in the world—not on the black market or in a museum or in a private collection or anywhere else. So they're all sitting out there somewhere, just waiting to be found. That was the project your uncle was working on for the Egyptian government. He had somehow gotten to the point where he actually had a map of some sort to where the stolen items were."

"And now he's dead," Deja said.

Right.

Now he's dead.

"So you can see what's at stake here," Alexandra said. "And

that's why I think you should get clear while you can."

Deja picked up a pebble and flicked it with her thumb.

"That's not going to happen, so get used to it."

21

Day Two—July 13
Tuesday Night

———————————

Pop. Pop. Pop. Durand stayed motionless behind the door and breathed through an open mouth. When the downstairs door opened and then slammed, he quickly but quietly went to the front window and pulled the curtain back ever so slightly. A shadowy figure carrying a suitcase was disappearing up the street on foot.

Durand exhaled.

Yeah, baby!

No one ever sees him.

Ever.

He was invisible.

Downstairs, the boxer was sprawled on the floor, with a bloody mess where his head should have been. The office was ransacked and the laptop was gone.

Freaky.

Suddenly the front doorknob jiggled violently and a gruff voice came from just beyond. "Hey! Are you okay in there?" Durand froze. "Bruno, try the back!"

Shit!

Out.

Out.

Out.

He needed to get out.

Now.

This second.

He ran to the back door and got there just as a man entered. They stared at each other, for just a heartbeat, and then Durand punched him in the face as hard as he could.

The man fell.

Durand jumped over him and ran as fast as he could into the night.

He zigzagged through the darkness, made it to his car and then got the hell out of there, actually encountering two cop cars speeding to the scene in the opposite direction. He had blood on his right fist, no doubt from the man's nose, and wiped it on his shirt as he drove.

He was safe now.

No problem.

Back home, he washed his hands, put all his clothes in a plastic garbage bag—every last stitch of them, right down to his socks—and threw them in a dumpster in an alley behind a car repair shop, a good two kilometers away.

Then he went back home and showered.

That's when he noticed something unexpected; his fist was bleeding, not much but a little.

He must have cut himself on the man's tooth when he punched him.

That meant his blood might be at the scene.

That wasn't good but wasn't worth worrying about. If it

was anywhere, it would be on the man's face. By now the guy had washed it off and it was long gone.

He uncorked a bottle of red wine, poured a glass over ice and then called the client as he sipped.

"It's late," the client said.

Yeah.

Durand knew that but he had run into a problem.

The client listened to what happened without interruption and then said, "Okay, you got a look at the guy who killed Trickett, right?"

"Right."

"Find out who he is. That's your next assignment."

"Why?"

"That's need-to-know," the client said. "Also, email me whatever it was that you got out of Trickett's laptop. Get a pencil, I'm going to give you the address."

Durand jotted it down and transmitted the files.

Then he pulled them up on his computer to see what was there.

Luc Trickett, who the hell are you?

And why does anyone care?

22

Day Two—July 13
Tuesday Night

A call to Rex in the afternoon confirmed that the caveman DJ would be playing tonight. The doors didn't open until 10:30 p.m., meaning an hour after Teffinger's bedtime, so he headed back to the hotel after supper with Fallon and crawled into bed for a nap. He woke when someone knocked on his door. No light seeped in the window, meaning night had come to Paris.

He looked at his watch.

9:30 p.m.

He opened the door expecting to find Fallon.

Instead it was Sophia, the curvy beauty from the front desk.

She pushed past him, bounced on the edge of the bed and said, "You promised me a drink."

He grunted.

"Your timing's bad," he said.

"Don't tell me you already have plans."

He nodded.

"I do, but that's not it," he said. "I sort of have a thing going on with someone."

"Here in Paris?"

"Yes."

"You've only been here two days," she said.

He knew that and said so.

"I'm jealous."

Teffinger chuckled.

"I got to get in the shower," he said.

"Go ahead," she said. "I'll just hang out. You want anything ironed, as long as I'm here?"

"No, don't bother."

"It's not a bother, just go take your shower."

He did, slightly worried that Sophia would suddenly pull the curtain back and step inside, but she didn't. He dried off and slipped his jeans on. When he came out, he saw something he could hardly believe, namely Sophia lying on her back on the bed, naked, with the lights off.

Her arms were stretched up high over her head and her hands gripped the bed railing.

She wiggled her hips and said, "Surprise."

Suddenly knuckles rapped on the door, the knob turned and someone walked into the room, someone wearing a short black skirt, a white blouse tied above her stomach, and black high heels.

Fallon.

She froze.

So did Teffinger.

So did Sophia.

Fallon looked at the woman, then Teffinger, then the woman, then Teffinger. He expected her to turn and slam the door on her way out. Instead she shut the door gently and asked,

"Who's your friend?"

Teffinger swallowed.

"Sophia."

"She's beautiful," Fallon said.

She walked over to the bed, sat down, and ran a finger on the woman's stomach, around her bellybutton. Sophia closed her eyes. Fallon straddled Sophia's hips and played with her nipples, for a long time, whipping the woman into a frenzy. Then she moved up until her thighs were on each side of the woman's face.

Sophia knew what to do.

She did it well.

Then Fallon reciprocated.

Sophia wanted to come to Rex with them, so they made a pit stop at her apartment. She took a five-minute shower and slipped into high heels and a short white dress with lots of cleavage. By eleven, they were inside the club, which was a high-energy pickup place jammed with a thousand beautiful people, throbbing bass and sexual tension.

Fallon and Sophia danced with each other.

Close.

Flirty.

With a lot of touching.

There were some things Teffinger could do and some he couldn't. Dancing was one of the things he couldn't unless he was drunk, so he got a beer, found a place against the wall, and studied the target.

Mister DJ.

Unfortunately, conditions couldn't have been worse—the cage was dark, the man moved around, hair hung over his face, and he wore sunglasses. For all Teffinger could tell, he could be the caveman or he could equally be the crazy airport cabbie with the gold tooth.

What was that guy's name?

Baptiste?

Yeah, that was it.

Baptiste.

Suddenly someone blew in his ear. He turned and found a woman staring at him, very close, almost touching, someone he didn't know.

Drop-dead gorgeous.

Wildly drunk.

Without saying a word, she kissed him on the lips, grabbed his hand and pulled him towards the dance floor like she owned him.

He almost went but didn't.

The woman muttered something in French and disappeared.

Fallon wandered over five minutes later, spotted him, and handed him a fresh beer, which he downed quicker than he should. Then they danced—close and hot and intimate. She gyrated hypnotically to the beat with her stomach and hips and arms while Teffinger ran his hands over her body, every inch of it.

Dangerously.

Inappropriately.

He didn't care what anyone saw or thought.

Neither did she.

Suddenly the DJ stepped out of his cage and headed for the restroom.

Teffinger grabbed Fallon's hand and said, "This is our chance," and they followed.

23

Day Three—July 14
Wednesday Morning

Deja went to work Wednesday morning as normal, as if she hadn't killed a man, as if she wasn't throat deep in a weird archeological hunt, as if she spent her evenings watching TV instead of sitting in the dark with a mysterious woman and a pair of binoculars. She drank coffee as usual. She knew the motions of her job and performed them well. Not even Yves Petit detected anything.

Yesterday's paper was in the kitchen.

A photograph of a murder suspect on page 5 had a slight resemblance to one of the attorneys on the thirty-first floor, a man named Paul Sabater.

But the resemblance was slight.

It clearly wasn't him.

It did, however, look like someone else she had seen somewhere.

Where?

She couldn't remember.

A bus driver?

She didn't care.

She had no dog in that fight.

Mid-morning her cell phone rang and Alexandra's voice came through. The woman sounded like she was strapped into a roller coaster and free-falling down the first hill. "I'm in the house!" she said.

"The looters' house?"

"Yes!"

"Are you nuts?"

"Just be quiet and listen because I don't know how much time I have," Alexandra said. "All of Remy's stuff is here, just like we thought. Here's the dilemma. If I take it, they'll know we have it and they'll hunt us to the ends of the earth to get it back. I don't mind the risk but I'm not going to put your life on the line without your consent."

Deja stood up and paced.

She didn't care about herself but did care about Alexandra.

"Are you there?" Alexandra asked.

Yes.

"I'm thinking."

"Well think fast."

"Is Remy's laptop there?"

It was.

At least, she assumed it was his.

"Are there any blank discs around?"

A beat then, "Yes."

"Copy his files and leave everything else for now," Deja said. "Whatever you do, don't let them catch you."

"I'll call you in fifteen minutes," Alexandra said.

The line went dead.

Alexandra actually called in thirteen. "Done deal," she said. "I'm safe, in my car, heading out."

Deja exhaled and wiped her forehead.

"You shouldn't have done that without a lookout," she said. "I thought we had an understanding."

They did but Alexandra drove by, saw an opportunity and got stupid.

"I don't think they're going to know I was there, but I'm going to rent us a place this afternoon, somewhere safe. We need to do that anyway. It's time. I'll call you later with directions. What I don't know is whether—"

She stopped talking.

"Alexandra, are you there?"

No response.

Deja checked her phone.

The connection was fine.

Then Alexandra's voice came through.

"There's a car behind me," she said. "I don't know if it's following me, or what. I'll call you later."

The connection died.

24

Day Three—July 14
Wednesday Morning

The files from Luc Trickett's laptop had nothing to do with Durand's client, nor did they provide any hints as to who killed the boxer or why. Durand went through everything twice, just to be sure, before he finally gave up.

Most of the files were porn.

The boxer apparently had a fetish for lesbians.

Young ones.

The younger, the better.

Borderline kiddie-porn.

Is that why he got killed?

Some irate father?

Durand scratched his head and decided he needed sunshine, needed it bad and needed it now. Fifteen minutes later he was at a café table on the sunny side of the street, drinking coffee and reading the paper. All the while, he kept pulling up an image of the woman from De Luna.

The blond with the tattoo.

Stretched out on the rack.

Blindfolded.

Caressed and tickled by strangers.

When the woman left de Luna Monday night, she left alone, and Durand followed.

He had to.

He stayed a good distance back.

Luckily, she didn't call a cab or get on the Metro. In hindsight, there was no need. It turned out that she lived on a houseboat, a short twenty minute walk from the club. Durand found a private nook in the darkness and watched the boat for an hour.

He rubbed his cock until he came, then got up and left.

That was Monday night.

Now it was Wednesday morning.

He finished his coffee, drank another cup, and then took the Metro over to the houseboat to see if the tattooed woman was out and about.

Maybe she was in a bikini, working on her tan, but that wasn't the case.

The boat was quiet with no signs of life, rocking gently from the wake of a barge.

He strolled down the cobblestone walkway, not more than five feet away, and diverted his eyes to the windows as he passed. The interior was nice, with lots of wood. But that's not what he cared about. He wanted to know if anyone lived there besides her.

He couldn't tell but at least he hadn't seen anyone so far.

That was good.

He was on a bench forty meters from the houseboat, enjoying

the sun, when his cell rang and the voice of the client came through. "Did you figure out who killed Luc Trickett yet?"

Durand chuckled.

"Not quite yet," he said. "My crystal ball is in the shop for maintenance." He got serious and added, "Some of the girls on his computer were pretty young, maybe under eighteen—maybe under sixteen. But I don't think that's why he's dead."

"Agreed," the client said. "Can you draw at all?"

Durand tossed a rock into the Seine.

"I'm no Michelangelo, but I've held a pencil or two on occasion. Why?"

"Why don't you see if you can sketch a picture of the guy and fax it to me, while everything's fresh in your mind."

Sure, why not?

He'd give it a try but couldn't give any promises as to the quality.

25

Day Three—July 14
Wednesday Morning

Teffinger woke before daybreak Wednesday morning, rolled onto his back with his eyes still closed, and remembered the insane sex with Fallon last night. He moved his hand over to be sure she was still there. She must have felt his touch because she said, "You up?"

He was.

"I'm going to go for a jog," he said.

"I'm coming with you."

'Really?"

"Don't worry," she said. "I'll go slow enough for you to keep up."

"Cute."

A slight chill hung in the morning air, but nothing like Denver. They crossed the bridge and ran on the islands where the traffic was thinner. The barges and Batobuses were still tied up somewhere in the dark, leaving the Seine smooth. The lights of Paris reflected off the black surface. Teffinger had always thought that Denver was a beautiful city, set at the base of the

Rocky Mountains. He now realized how wrong he had been. It was nothing compared to Paris. Being here made him realize how sheltered and uncultured his life had been.

He pictured himself living here, maybe not even returning to Denver at all. Targaux seemed to like him. Maybe he'd find a way to bring Teffinger on board if he lived here and learned a little French. If not that, Fallon mentioned she had connections with INTERPOL. Maybe she could get him hooked up there.

Or maybe he'd join the FBI or CIA.

Or, hell, just float on his savings for a year.

Maybe get out of the crime business altogether.

He could live on the boat with Fallon and spend the weekends with her in the museums.

He'd pick up the paintbrushes again.

Live a little.

See Paris through Fallon's eyes and taste it with her mouth.

Take holidays in Amsterdam and London and Vienna; and other places he had never been to or even knew about. Maybe he would take a one-year sabbatical from his job instead of quitting. Then if things didn't work out, he'd just go back, none the worse for a few new experiences.

He looked at Fallon jogging beside him.

So hypnotic.

So sensuous.

So frail.

What would she think of the idea? Would she go for it? She probably would. She had let Teffinger get a hold of her, deep down, and she wanted more—he could tell. True, she was wild, but there was another part of her that longed to be tame.

Needed to be.

She had chosen Teffinger for that project.

He could feel it down in his soul.

They jogged another mile, slower now, slow enough to talk. Teffinger said, "I didn't know you were bi."

She looked over.

"You mean Sophia?"

Right.

Sophia.

"That was the first time I ever did anything like that," she said.

"Really?"

"Yes. ¡Did you enjoy the show?"

"To tell you the truth, I was a little jealous."

She tossed her hair and smiled.

"Good."

Teffinger dropped Fallon off at the houseboat and then headed to the hotel to shower and change. Tracy White's roommate, Michelle Berri, had been missing for more than four days at this point.

Not good.

Statistically, she was dead.

And the hunt so far had been nonproductive.

They finally got a good look at the DJ last night when he went to the restroom. He might be the caveman, but he just as easily might not. It was too hard to tell with the long hair and the goatee. Even worse, after getting two phone tips early Tuesday morning, they dried up. Not a single additional call came in yesterday, even though the caveman's sketch had been broadcast on every TV channel both in the afternoon and the evening.

They better come up with something real brilliant, real fast. Meaning today.

When he swung back to the houseboat to pick up Fallon, something was visibly wrong.

"What's going on?" he asked.

She sat down on the couch, got lost momentarily in thought, and said, "I did it. I shouldn't be surprised. I knew I was going to do it, but now that it's actually done, it feels a lot more serious than I expected."

Teffinger had a pretty good idea what she was talking about but needed to be sure.

"Did what?" he asked.

"Someone called the office and said he was with INTERPOL," Fallon said. "He said they might have a similar eyes-gouged-out case in Greece and wanted to talk to the Paris witness, the one who gave the sketch that's all over the news. The office patched that call through to me, but didn't give the guy my name, which is standard protocol. I told the guy that the witness was someone named Fallon Le Rue, where she lived and her phone number, my land line, not my cell. He said, Thanks. I waited for ten minutes and didn't get a call. Then I phoned one of my contacts at INTERPOL and asked her if they were working on a case in Greece." She paused, looked Teffinger in the eyes and said, "They aren't."

"So he did the exact same thing he did in Denver," Teffinger said.

Fallon nodded.

"The bait is set," she said. "And I'm it."

Her lips trembled.

She stood up and hugged Teffinger tight.

Teffinger hugged her back and cursed himself for ever

coming up with such a stupid idea.

26

Day Three—July 14
Wednesday Afternoon

The vehicle behind Alexandra followed for five kilometers before it mysteriously veered off and disappeared. Alexandra immediately called Deja and said, "I think it was them, there were two guys in the car. They must have seen me leaving and thought I took their files. My guess is that while they were keeping me in sight, someone else went through the house, didn't find anything missing and then called them up and said to abort. In hindsight, it's a good thing I didn't take anything; otherwise I'd be dead right now. That means that's the second time you saved my life."

"Yeah, well, return the favor someday."

Alexandra exhaled.

"Hopefully I'll never get the chance. I'm going to zigzag around until I'm positive they're gone. Then I'm going to rent a hotel room and see what's on Remy's disk."

"Pay cash," Deja said.

"Huh?"

"For the hotel room, pay cash instead of using a credit card.

We don't know how sophisticated these people are."

Right.

Cash.

Good idea.

Alexandra picked Deja up at the end of the day. They took the Metro into the Invalides and Eiffel Tower Quarter where they got on a Batobus. That took them up the Seine, across from the Ile St. Louis, where they got off and walked north on Rue Vieille Du Temple into the boutiques, cafes, art galleries and narrow streets of the Marais district in the northeast corner of Paris, a high-rent trendy place.

Deja knew the area well.

A couple of gay friends lived on Rue St. Giles.

The hotel room was nice.

Too nice.

Deja must have had a look in her eyes because Alexandra said, "Relax. The government's paying for it. We deserve a little luxury after spending a night on the grass. I've been studying Remy's disk all day. Like I said before, there was no map in there. I did a search to find all files that had been generated or updated in the last six months, after the tomb was discovered. Most of those files were just cryptic notes—lists of things to do and stuff like that. But as I started to go through them, I think I figured out what Remy's theory was."

Deja pulled off her shoes, flopped down on the bed and stretched out.

"So what was it?"

Alexandra pulled the curtains shut. "Just in case," she said. "Remy's theory—if I'm piecing it together right—was that a wealthy man orchestrated the robbery of the tomb."

Deja wrinkled her brow, confused.

"Why would he think that?" she questioned. "I would think just the opposite, namely that a pack of lowlife thieves did it."

"First of all, what a lot of laypeople don't appreciate is that it wasn't just royalty who mummified the dead," Alexandra said. "Private citizens did too, but only the wealthy ones, because only they could afford it. Mummification was the way to ensure the transformation from death to immortality. Private persons had just as much desire as royalty did to see the ones they loved live forever."

That made sense; perfect sense actually.

"Remy's theory appears to be that there was a death in the family of a wealthy private person very close in time to the death of the pharaoh. Probably a son. To maximize the chances for the son's immortality, the wealthy man employed the services of several men—probably his servants—to rob the tomb of the pharaoh. Then he included those items in the mummification of his son."

Deja scratched her head.

"So if we figure out who this wealthy man was, and where he buried his son, then we have our treasure."

Alexandra nodded.

"If it's true that Remy had a map," she said, "it must show the location of the son's burial site. Somehow Remy figured out who the man was and where his son was buried. Unfortunately, those matters aren't discussed in any of his computer files. What we need to do is get our hands on the source documents that Remy was studying before he died. That's how he got his answers and that's how we'll get ours."

Deja sat up and cocked her head.

"The looters have those," she said.

Yes, they did.

"Which means we need to get back into that house," Alexandra said.

"You're kidding, right?"

No.

She wasn't.

"Tonight," she added.

27

Day Three—July 14
Wednesday Afternoon

Marcel Durand didn't have a lot of friends. Not because he couldn't, but because he didn't want them
or need them. He had his P.I. work and his money.
People who weren't his clients or critical to his investigations
were, for the most part, baggage that didn't do much except
clutter up his life. He did, however, tolerate a few people.

Anton Fornier was one of them; taxi driver in the day, a
hitman at night, a man with a slight caveman edge.

Durand spotted him parked outside the Hotel de Sille,
wandered over, stuck his head in the window and said, "They
need better security around here. Even people from prehistoric
times are getting in."

Anton looked up, ready for confrontation, but the corner
of his mouth turned up ever so slightly when he saw who it
was. "I'll be damned," he said. "It's been—how long?—two or
three years?"

"At least," Durand said. "You whacked the beard off. I
wouldn't have recognized you if it hadn't been for the cab."

They chatted while Anton waited for his fare. Then Durand lowered his voice and asked the question he was curious about, "So, how's the contract business?"

Anton's eyes darted, as if searching for cops.

Then he said, "It's been slow, actually. I've got one on the horizon though, as soon as they can figure out the target's name."

"What does that mean?"

"It means they know they're going to kill him, but haven't figured out who he is yet," Anton said.

"Why? What'd the guy do?"

"He killed a woman," Anton said. "He put a plastic bag over her head and duct-taped it around her neck. Then he sat back and watched the air run out."

Durand pictured it and said, "Nice guy."

Anton made a face and grunted.

Madonna's "Like A Prayer" came from a parked car.

The fare shuffled out of the hotel wrestling with two suitcases. Anton popped the trunk, stepped out and ran over to assist, wearing his best smile, already posturing for the tip. Durand waved goodbye, headed across the street and shouted over his shoulder, "Give me a call when you feel like getting drunk."

Anton looked up and chuckled.

"That's every five minutes," he shouted back.

The fare—an elderly woman—froze.

Anton took the suitcase out of her hand, put it in the trunk and said, "I'm just messing around. You're fine." When the worry washed off the woman's face, Anton slammed the lid, held the door open for her and said, "I'm not a drunk. I'm actually a killer."

She looked stunned.

Then she shook her head at her own gullibility and said, "Got me."

Durand turned, ran back across the street and pulled Anton to the side. "Hey," he said, "I just thought of something. If they need help figuring out who this guy is, I'd be happy to assist. That's what I do, remember."

Anton nodded.

"I'll mention it."

"You do that."

He watched Anton pull off, walked down to the Seine, crossed the bridge to the Right Bank, and took a spot on a bench. Eight or ten pigeons flew over and strutted their tail feathers until they got no food. Durand studied the houseboat moored on the opposite side of the river.

It was a nice unit.

Pricey.

Clearly the tattoo woman wasn't hurting for money.

So why was she down at De Luna, stretched out on a rack, getting felt up and tickled for a few measly euros?

There was only one possible explanation.

She liked it.

Little Miss Kinky.

Durand looked at his watch and found it was later than he thought. He went home, sketched the face of the man who turned the boxer's head into hamburger last night, and faxed the sketch to his client.

The client called two minutes later.

"Is this pretty accurate?"

"Within reason," Durand said. "Do you know him?"

"No."

28

Day Three—July 14
Wednesday Afternoon

———————

The bait was set, like it or not. The most important thing in the world right now, at least from Teffinger's point of view, was that Fallon not be hurt or killed. So they fired up the coffee maker and spent a solid hour on the boat, going over vantage points, movements and plans of defense. At the end, Teffinger should have felt better, but didn't because Fallon was insistent that she be the one to kill the man if it came to it.

"I'm positioned to handle the fallout, you're not," she said.

He grunted.

"Screw fallout, but that's not the issue," he said. "The issue is, we need him alive. He's our only link to Michelle Berri."

Fallon wrinkled her forehead.

"I forgot all about that." She studied him and asked, "Have you ever killed anyone?"

Memories flashed.

"Yes," he said. "Have you?"

She shook her head.

"No."

"It's more serious than you think," he said, "even when you're in the right."

She picked a lighter off the counter, flicked a flame and looked at him through it. Then she shut it down and said, "I won't lose any sleep if he makes me do it. Trust me."

Teffinger heard the words but didn't process them.

Instead he picked her up, carried her downstairs, threw her on the bed and pulled her pants and panties off. Nothing else, just her pants and panties.

Then he took her.

Hard.

Passionate.

Like a caveman.

They headed to the office to see if any phone tips had come in. On the way, Teffinger had a wild idea, got the number for Les Taxis Bleus and dialed.

A woman answered.

Teffinger explained that a cab driver with a gold tooth picked him up at the airport Monday morning, a talkative man named Baptiste. Teffinger wanted to know if there was a way to get in touch with the man. He needed to talk to him about something.

The woman on the other end took Teffinger's phone number.

"I'll give him a message," she said. "No guarantees he'll call."

"Thanks."

Teffinger hung up, looked at Fallon and said, "He'll call."

"How do you know?"

"Because I gave him a good tip."

Two minutes later, Baptiste called.

"You're the American," he said. "I remember you. You were the scared one."

"Not scared," Teffinger said, "just not used to Paris driving."

Baptiste chuckled.

"Scared," he repeated.

Teffinger grunted.

"Okay, maybe a little."

Then he explained that he was looking for a favor. "Check out page 5 of yesterday's paper. You'll see a sketch of a man. Someone said he might be a taxi driver. I'm trying to find out if that's true or not and wondered if you knew him."

Five minutes later, Baptiste dialed back.

"That could be Anton Fornier," he said.

Anton Fornier?

Right.

Anton Fornier.

"Thanks, I owe you one."

"You already gave me ten," Baptiste said, referring to euros. "Now we're even. You take care, American."

"You too, Frenchman."

Baptiste laughed, then hung up.

At Fallon's office, the coffee was hot but the news was bad. No more calls had come in on the sketch. Fallon ran a background check on their new cabbie friend, Anton Fornier.

A couple of minor things, that's all he had.

She looked at Teffinger and said, "So now what?"

29

Day Three—July 14
Wednesday Night

———————

The Paris sky got cloudy Wednesday evening and then dropped rain shortly after dark—nothing heavy, but constant. Deja and Alexandra made a slow pass by the looters' house, which came in and out of focus through sweeping wipers.

The interior was dark.

No cars were in the driveway.

"We might be in luck," Deja said.

She expected Alexandra to agree but no agreement came.

Instead the woman said, "It smells like a trap."

Trap.

The word made Deja shiver, so much so that she jumped when her cell phone rang. It turned out to be Nicholas Ringer. "I just thought I'd give you a call and let you know I haven't forgotten about you," he said.

"Anything new?"

"No," Ringer said. "Unfortunately, the P.I. got sidetracked onto some urgent matter for another client."

"When is he going to get back on it?"

Ringer exhaled.

"I don't know," he said. "I tried to light a fire but he warned me that this other matter was really urgent. So we'll see. I'll keep the pressure on."

Okay.

Thanks again.

When Deja hung up, Alexandra asked, "Who was that?"

Deja debated whether to tell the woman or not.

"Okay," she said, "I'm going to tell you something, but don't freak out."

Freak out?

Why would she freak out?

What's going on?

"That was a man named Nicholas Ringer. He owns a ship-yard and is a client of the law firm I work at," Deja said. "We got to talking a couple of days ago when he was at the firm getting some work done. It came up that Remy got murdered. It turns out that Mr. Ringer had an archeological class with Remy ten or twelve years ago, when he was going to the university. He offered to hire a P.I. to investigate Remy's murder if the police didn't make progress. Later that day my apartment got broken into and you showed up out of the blue. I thought that was a pretty big coincidence."

Okay.

"Anyway, I called Mr. Ringer up and asked if he could put a P.I. on you, just to see if you were legit," Deja said.

"On me?"

"Right."

"You had me investigated?"

"Like I said, don't freak out," Deja said. "You checked out

and it's a done deal."

Alexandra grunted.

"I can't believe you did that."

"Like I said, it's a done deal."

"Didn't you trust me?"

"I did and I do," Deja said. "It was just so weird that Remy got killed, my place got trashed and you showed up at the door, eager to protect me. I didn't know if the whole thing was a charade to get my confidence to see if I had the map and would give it to you."

Silence.

"I didn't know you then like I do now," Deja added. "We didn't have any history together yet."

More silence.

Then Alexandra said, "Who was the P.I. that got hired? Do you know?"

Yes.

She did.

"Someone named Marcel Durand."

Durand, huh?

Right.

"Tell me about Nicholas Ringer."

Deja told her what she knew, which drew a lot of questions. Then she asked, "Are you mad at me?"

Alexandra exhaled.

"I would be, except for that little incident where you saved my life."

Deja grinned.

They made another pass by the house.

Then another.

Nothing changed.

The structure was dark and creepy, exactly the way it would be if someone was laying a trap, or if no one was home. They parked several streets over, more than a kilometer away, doubled back on foot, and took a position in the shadows across the street.

The plan was simple.

They would get in phone contact. Alexandra would go in and keep her ear to the phone. Deja would stay outside and be the lookout.

"See you in hell," Alexandra said.

Then she headed for the structure, looked in the side windows, and disappeared around the back corner. "I'm at the back door," she said. "Nothing suspicious so far. I'm going to shine the flashlight in."

Silence.

"It looks clear," she said. "I'm going in."

Glass busted.

"Okay, I'm in." A moment passed. "There's something wrong."

"What?"

"I don't know. It just doesn't feel right."

"Get out of there," Deja said.

Silence.

"Alexandra?"

Silence.

"Alexandra, are you there?"

30

Day Three—July 14
Wednesday Night

After dark, Durand stuffed cuffs, rope, duct tape, latex gloves, a mask, a ball gag and a pair of binoculars in a black nylon backpack. He dressed in his best stalking clothes, all dark, and sheathed an 8-inch serrated knife on his belt. Then he headed to his car and drove through a light but persistent drizzle as the Stone's "Paint it Black" spilled from the radio. Twenty minutes later, he parked on a side street, got out, and walked for a kilometer through a wet Paris night.

That brought him to the Seine, on the opposite side of the river from the houseboat, a hundred meters down.

The weather worked through his clothes and chilled his brain, but it also kept the Parisians off the streets. He looked around, saw no one, and slipped into the deeper shadows of a clump of trees next to a retaining wall. The binoculars came out and pulled the houseboat in. The window coverings were all closed but the lights were on. An occasional shadowy movement indicated that the woman was home.

Good.

Durand pulled up an image of her body.

Her tattoo.

Her face.

He sat down, leaned against the wall and felt the rain start to seep through the hood. Minute after drizzly minute passed. An hour later, the lights inside the boat went out. He studied the vessel through the binoculars for another thirty minutes and saw nothing to indicate that the woman had done anything except go to bed.

He stood up, hunched against the weather, and headed that way.

Game time.

He got to the bridge, crossed the river and inched his way towards the target, one silent step at a time.

Slowly.

Watching.

Listening.

He stopped next to the boat with a racing heart as he looked for the best place to step aboard.

Do it carefully.

Don't rock the stupid thing.

Don't wake her up.

Suddenly his cell phone rang. At that second, he remembered he had forgotten to mute it. Damn it! He flicked it open before it could ring again, but didn't answer. Instead, he punched the power off and watched the display fade to black.

He stood there, frozen.

If the woman heard it, she would suspect something. It had been too close to the boat. No one should be there this late at night, especially in the rain.

He stood still, waiting to see if a light turned on or if a window cover pulled back.

Nothing happened and the pounding in his heart dialed down just a touch.

He almost stepped aboard but his instincts brought his foot to a standstill.

They told him to leave.

To watch the boat from across the river.

To play it safe.

To come back in an hour.

He headed down the walkway, briskly but silently, already knowing he had made the right decision. Thirty steps later, he turned and looked over his shoulder, just to make sure everything was okay. To his shock a man was behind him, a large man, charging full speed on silent feet.

Durand got the knife in hand and stabbed with all his might as the man lunged through the air at him.

31

Teffinger woke Thursday morning with a headache, a dry mouth and an empty feeling. The first two were the product of too much beer. The empty part came from the fact that the guy got away last night and because of that Michelle Berri was still out there somewhere in the world.

It was Teffinger's fault.

He shook his head and still couldn't believe it.

He had the guy right there in his sights but he lunged too early and planted his face in the ground.

He never even got a look at the guy.

The good news was that the man's knife landed between Teffinger's arm and his body. It sliced the side of his chest, but didn't land six inches over in his heart. The wound was superficial enough that Fallon treated it. After that, they abandoned the houseboat and headed to Teffinger's hotel room where it would be safer. They were too wound up to sleep and ended up in a bar.

Fallon drank wine.

Teffinger drank beer.

Cold beer.

Something in a brown bottle with a French label.

Beer that went down too smooth and too fast.

Beer that now pounded with little hammers inside his skull.

He popped three aspirins and took a hot shower. When he got out, Fallon the angel handed him a cup of hot coffee and asked, "How's the cut?" He raised his arm to show her. She frowned and added, "It's still bleeding. You need stitches."

He raked sopping wet hair back with his fingers, took a long slurp from the cup, and checked the wound in the mirror.

True, it was bleeding, but not much.

Not enough to waste time on.

"I'm starved," he said. "Let's get some breakfast—my treat."

She chuckled.

"Teffinger, you just referred to yourself and the words my treat in the same sentence. Now I really am worried about you."

He put a puzzled look on his face.

"Are you serious? Did I just really do that?"

She nodded.

"I was hoping today would be a better one than yesterday," he said, "but I've only been up fifteen minutes and I'm already making mistakes."

The cab driver, Anton Fornier, didn't work on Thursdays and Fridays. Teffinger and Fallon sat inside a coffee bar across the street from the man's apartment, waiting for him to wake up and make a move.

Maybe lead them to Michelle Berri.

They found out a few things about him yesterday, other than he looked like a caveman. He was a good driver with no accidents or customer complaints. He worked the day shift now, meaning he wasn't on duty Friday night when Tracy White got her eyes gouged out and Michelle Berri got taken.

Opportunity.

He had only been with the Les Taxis Bleus for nine months, so they had no records as to whether Fornier was in France when Amanda Peterson got her eyes gouged out in Denver.

More opportunity, possibly.

Most importantly, however, he lived above his means.

Somehow, someway, he had money in his pocket that he shouldn't.

That's what got Teffinger's attention more than anything.

Teffinger took a sip of coffee and said, "It's too bad I didn't at least get a punch in last night. If the DJ or our friend Mr. Cab Driver was walking around with a black eye today, that would eliminate a lot of work."

She nodded.

"Next time, don't spend all your energy attacking his knife with your body."

Teffinger smiled.

"So what else are you working on, besides this?"

She shrugged.

"Investigation-wise, this is it," she said. "Except for one cold case."

"Cold cases are the worst," Teffinger said. "Tell me about it."

"There's not that much to tell," she said. "Some guy put a plastic bag over a woman's head and duct-taped it around her neck. Then he sat back and watched the air run out."

Teffinger winced.

"How long ago?"

"A year," she said. "It was actually my first case." She raised the coffee to her lips, took a sip and studied his eyes over the edge. "Tell me about Denver. Do you have a girlfriend waiting for you?"

No.

He didn't.

"Five girlfriends?"

He grinned.

No.

"A dog?"

No.

"Nothing."

Just his job.

"Then maybe you should stay in Paris," she said. Suddenly something outside got her attention and made her put the coffee cup down. "We're up."

Teffinger looked across the street and saw the cab driver, Anton Fornier.

32

Day Four—July 15
Thursday Morning

D eja and Alexandra woke Thursday morning before
dawn, showered, and headed for the nearest place
that sold caffeine and croissants. Last night had
been good in that the looters weren't lurking inside with the
lights off as part of a trap. But it had been bad in that they had
abandoned the house and had taken all of Remy's research and
papers with them.

Gone.

Gone.

Gone.

There were two possible explanations.

They might be worried about the police finding Pascal Lambert's body and then showing up at the man's house as part of
an investigation.

Or they might have found the map and headed to Egypt.

"Either way," Alexandra said, "we're screwed."

That was last night.

Deja hoped she'd be in a cheerier mood this morning.

The sleep and the coffee helped but not as much as she hoped.

Alexandra took a long slurp of coffee, got serious, and looked at Deja. "Do you have a passport?"

Deja nodded and already knew where the question was headed.

"What are you saying? Egypt?"

Alexandra nodded.

"I don't see any other options at this point," she said. "We'll never get our hands on Remy's source documents. Our only hope now is to recreate his footsteps. We know what his theory was. And we know that his last trip was to Cairo. That was the trip that you said he got all excited about."

Right.

It was.

"That's where he found what he was looking for," Alexandra said. "So if we're going to find it, that's where we need to be."

Yves Petit frowned when Deja told him she needed to take an emergency trip to Cairo.

She was too important to be gone.

"What's in Cairo?"

She was sorry.

She couldn't tell him.

It was a private matter.

"I'll still work eight hours a day or whatever it takes," she said. "I'll be fully accessible 24/7 by email and phone. You won't get a drop in either the quality or quantity of my work. I promise."

He studied her.

"I don't know what's going on," he said. "But if there's anything I can do—money or support or whatever—just say it."

Deja hugged him.

"All I need for you to do right now is indulge me."

He patted her on the back.

"Consider yourself indulged. And don't worry about work. Just take the time off."

She was almost out of his office when she turned and said, "There is one more thing you can do. Don't tell anyone where I am. Especially if someone calls up trying to find me."

He nodded.

"I won't even tell anyone in the office," he said.

33

Day Four—July 15
Thursday Morning

Marcel Durand woke Thursday morning to bad news, very bad news, namely a sketch of his face in the newspaper and an article reporting that he was a suspect in the murder of a man named Luc Trickett.

A picture of the victim was also shown.

The boxer.

Damn it!

The neighbor at the back door—the one Durand had to punch in the face and jump over Tuesday night after someone mangled the boxer's head with bullets—must have gotten a better look at Durand than he thought. Too bad he didn't know it then. He would have kicked the guy's eyes out.

He studied the sketch harder and the more he did, the better he felt.

He knew it was him but doubted anyone else would.

The likeness was remote, at best.

Just to be safe, though, he pulled out a pair of scissors, stepped to the mirror and chopped his hair.

Then he went out and bought a bottle of dye.

Raven black.

An hour later even he didn't recognize himself.

Then he called his client and told him about the development. "Don't worry about it," the client said. "If it ends up getting intense, I'll vouch that you were on a project for me. In the meantime, find the guy who killed the boxer."

The client chuckled, as if he just heard a joke.

"What?" Durand asked.

"I mean, your life is actually pretty sweet when you stop and think about it. You're getting paid to find the one person who can get you out of a mess."

Durand saw the irony but wasn't amused.

He took his ordinary forgettable face outside for a walk under the Paris sun and shifted his thinking to the tattooed woman with the houseboat, Fallon Le Rue.

Durand had been lucky last night.

The man chasing him either slipped on the wet pavement or made a mistake in the dark by lunging too soon.

Good thing, either way.

The man was strong and intense.

Where did he come from?

That was the big question.

Was he just some passerby who saw Durand acting suspicious? Was he inside the boat, sleeping with the woman, heard the cell phone ring and ran out? Or was he someone hiding in the shadows, actually expecting Durand to show up?

He kept walking.

The Paris sky was perfect.

So was the temperature.

The city buzzed.

He made a quick stop at a café bar, got an espresso to go, and sipped as he headed farther south. Suddenly something happened that he didn't expect. Several police cars were parked up ahead. Durand crossed to the other side of the street as he walked past.

What he saw he could hardly believe.

The cops were in the alley, at a dumpster, pulling out a black plastic bag—the very same bag that Durand stuffed his bloody clothes in after he left the boxer's house.

Damn it!

34

The cab driver—Anton Fornier—made his way to the Luxembourg Quarter in the southern section of Paris, where the buzz was slightly less intense, the chestnut trees were more plentiful and the crowd was younger.

There must be a university nearby.

He disappeared into a nice house on Rue Erasme Brossolette. Teffinger raked his hair back with his fingers and said, "What's a cab driver doing in a place like that?"

"I know that house," Fallon said.

"Really?"

"It's the headquarters of an international sex operation called Blue Moon."

"What kind of sex operation?"

"Escorts," Fallon said. "Very pricey escorts."

"How pricey?"

"Five thousand a night, or more," she said. "For that you get the best of the best. They recruit the women from all over—London, Munich, Vienna, you name it."

Teffinger shook his head.

"Five thousand," he said. "I can't even imagine. Why would anyone in the world pay that kind of money for a few minutes of pleasure?"

"Because the women are gorgeous and they're willing to get kinky," Fallon said.

"Kinky, huh?"

Yes.

Kinky.

Very kinky.

Fallon cocked her head and said, "Have you ever paid for it?"

"What do you think?"

"I think not."

"Okay, then, that's my answer."

She punched his arm.

"Come on, have you?"

"And I'm sticking to it," Teffinger said. "Five thousand is a lot of money. More than a cabbie can afford, that's for sure. So what the hell is our friend doing there?"

Good question.

"Want to know how I know about this place?" Fallon asked.

Yes.

He did.

He did indeed.

"It actually involves that cold case I was telling you about this morning," she said. "The woman who got smothered was someone named Sharla DePaglia. She worked for our friends in the house over there."

Meaning what?

She was an escort?

Fallon nodded.

"We were pretty sure she was working at the time she got murdered and that the person who did it was a Blue Moon client. But the company wouldn't cooperate."

Teffinger grunted.

"Bastards," he said.

"Bitches, actually," Fallon said. "Blue Moon is owned and operated by two sisters—Anastasie and Emmanuelle Atwood."

Teffinger paced.

"Maybe our cab driver friend is the one who killed your cold case woman."

Fallon shook her head.

"No, that would be too easy," she said. "My life doesn't work like that."

Five minutes after he went inside, Anton Fornier the taxi driver came back out and walked north. Teffinger and Fallon followed fifty steps behind.

"Well, he wasn't there for a session."

"They don't do them there. They do them offsite."

"Where?"

"Wherever the client wants," Fallon said. "That's part of the reason it's so pricey. The women have to go into an uncontrolled and unsupervised environment."

"And get kinky at the same time," Teffinger added.

Exactly.

"No wonder they end up dead. I wonder if Mr. Cab Man was laying five big ones on the table just now and arranging for a session. Maybe he was looking at pictures of the women who were available tonight. Reading the menu."

"That makes sense," Fallon said. "But where does he get the money?"

Teffinger grunted.

"That's a question I'm getting more and more interested in," he said. "Tell me more about your cold case. I'm starting to get the feeling it's somehow connected to Tracy White and Michelle Berri."

"Why?"

"Because Tracy White is connected to a caveman and a caveman is connected to Blue Moon. Tracy White died an ugly death. So did your cold-case woman—"

"—Sharla DePaglia."

"It could be the same person."

"That's thin."

Fallon filled him in as they walked. The victim, Sharla De-Paglia, was a wild-since-birth brunette bombshell from Rome. Her cell phone records showed numerous calls to and from Blue Moon, starting a week before she came to Paris. She had only been in town five days before she got murdered.

So sad.

"The guy tied her up in a standing spread-eagle position in a vacant building that was being renovated," Fallon said. "The construction workers found her like that the following morning, with a bag over her head, duct-taped around her neck."

"The little freak," Teffinger said.

"Here's the weird part," Fallon said. "There was a second set of ropes both up top and down below, empty. We believe that there was another woman hanging there spread-eagle with the victim."

"So he had two women?"

"Yes," Fallon said. "One he killed and one he let go."

"Why'd he let one go?"

She shrugged.

"The best we can figure is that he was playing some kind of a death game with them. The loser gets killed and the winner doesn't."

Teffinger frowned.

"I've seen some freaky things, but that's right up there."

Yes.

It was.

"But the good news is that you have a witness out there somewhere," Teffinger added.

Right, except they haven't been able to locate her and she probably wouldn't talk even if they did.

35

Day Four—July 15
Thursday Evening

———————

Deja and Alexandra touched down at Cairo International Airport just as the sun dipped below the western curvature of the earth. Heat radiated from every pore of every square inch of sand and rock and asphalt and building and vehicle and human being and dog in the city.

Deja pulled her hair into a ponytail and said, "How can anyone live here?"

Alexandra chuckled.

"This? This is nothing, this is an arctic ice storm," she said. "Enjoy it while you can. Tomorrow is going to be a lot hotter." Deja must have had a look of disbelief on her face because Alexandra added, "I'm serious."

They hopped in a cab.

It headed into traffic that got more aggressive and dangerous as they got deeper into the throes of the city. On the way, Alexandra explained a few things. "Cairo has over 17 million people. It's 90 percent Muslim, so most of the women will have their faces covered, at least when they're in public or in the presence of a man. The women who don't cover up are either non-Muslims or tourists. Egypt is still very much a caste system, with women finishing a distant second. Men are still allowed to have more than one wife and a lot of them do."

"You're kidding, right?"

Wrong.

She wasn't.

"Some have three, four, or even more. Since we won't be in traditional Muslim dress, men will try to figure out where we're from. It's not uncommon for them to propose almost immediately to an American woman, because they think all Americans are rich. Don't be surprised if someone comes up and offers you a thousand camels to marry him."

They came to a major intersection.

The cabbie paid attention, serious attention.

"Where are the traffic lights?" Deja asked.

The cabbie skirted through, narrowly avoiding getting clipped. "There aren't that many," Alexandra said. "It's basically first come, first serve. Whoever's the least afraid of dying has the right of way."

"Nice."

They checked into a hotel that was safe enough to not be killed in and slightly less hot than outside when they blasted the air conditioner on full.

Deja took a cold shower.

There.

Better.

Almost human again.

When she got out, Alexandra was in bed on top of the sheets, wearing a T-shirt and panties, with the lights out and her head in a pillow. "Get some sleep, darling," she said. "Tomorrow's going to be a long day."

36

Day Four—July 15
Thursday

Durand headed home from the police scene at the dumpster and thought about getting out of France. Even though he didn't kill the boxer, the police now had Durand's bag of clothes in addition to a witness placing him at the scene. Those clothes had both Durand's blood on them together with the blood of the back door guy that Durand had to punch.

Not good.

If the police somehow got Durand's name—say a call from someone who recognized him from the newspaper—they would have both a witness and physical evidence tying him to the scene.

Sure, he had an excuse.

It wasn't me.

It was someone else in the house the same time as me.

"Yeah, right. Maybe it was my mother. Is she the one who did it? Wait right here, I'm going to call her in for questioning, the little bitch—"

What to do?

Disappear to Amsterdam?

London?

Madrid?

Suddenly someone knocked on the door.

The cops?

Durand looked through the peephole, exhaled when he saw the cabbie-slash-hitman Anton Fornier and let him in. The man did a double-take on Durand's hair and said, "Do you have any idea how lucky you are to have a friend like me?"

Why?

What'd he do?

"I paid a visit to my client this morning, the one who's going to hire me for that hit I was telling you about," Fornier said.

"On the guy who smothered the woman?"

Right.

That guy.

"Anyway," Fornier said, "I conveyed your offer to help find the guy. And I vouched for you. I told them you could be trusted and knew how to keep your mouth shut. They're going to think about it." The man grinned. "I'm pretty sure they're going to go for it."

Durand slapped him on his back.

"Way to go."

Fornier got serious.

"If you get it, don't just spin your wheels and take their money," he said. "Remember, I don't get anything out of it unless you actually find the guy."

Durand nodded.

Understood.

"You know I'll do my best," he said. "And I'll tell you what

I'll do. If it turns out that I can't find the guy, I'll kick over to you a third of everything I get paid, for getting me the gig."

Fornier smiled ever so slightly.

"Fair enough," he said. "But find the guy." On the way out the door he turned. "What'd you do to your hair?"

"It's a long story."

Fornier wrinkled his forehead.

"It looks weird."

Fornier was almost gone when Durand said, "Hey, wait a minute. What's the woman's name?—the one who got smothered."

"Why?"

"I need to be sure I don't have a conflict."

Fornier hesitated.

Then said, "Your only conflict is the same as mine, meaning the check doesn't clear." He paused and added, "Sharla De-Paglia, that's her name."

"She sounds Italian."

"She's from Rome but got killed here," Fornier said. "Take care, my friend."

"You too."

37

Day Four—July 15
Thursday Morning

Teffinger and Fallon followed the caveman taxi driver, Anton Fornier, from Blue Moon to an apartment building and waited down the street. "Now what's he up to?" Fallon asked.

Teffinger shrugged.

"He could be a Blue Moon pimp."

"Meaning what, exactly?"

"He feels out his passengers, connects the promising ones to Blue Moon and gets a kickback," Teffinger said. "Or he could be a mule, meaning someone who collects the money from clients and takes it to Blue Moon. That makes sense in a way, because most guys aren't going to write a check or use a credit card. Nor are they going to want to be seen knocking on Blue Moon's door to make a cash payment. But there's no suspicion attached to taking a taxi ride. Then they get to trust the caveman and shorten things up by letting him knock on their door and make a pickup. Either way, the caveman gets in the middle of the action. That would explain his mystery money."

Fallon studied him.

"You have a seriously devious mind," she said.

Teffinger nodded.

He was about to say, You have no idea, but spotted something that looked like a public restroom a half-block down the street and said, "Is that what I think it is?"

"That depends on what you think it is."

He headed that way.

"I'm going to check it out."

"Hold on," she said, and gave him a couple of coins. "You'll need these."

Teffinger's suspicion was correct. It wasn't just a standalone public restroom, but an insanely modern one. For a few small coins, the door opened and he got up to fifteen minutes in a very clean place. A sign warned that after fifteen minutes, the door would automatically open and an automated sanitation process would begin. Teffinger didn't need fifteen minutes. He only needed one.

"I love this town," he told Fallon. "It's like someone designed it around me."

She smiled.

"We had too many people marking their territory before these," she said, "especially at night."

Teffinger chuckled as if he just heard a joke.

"What?"

"This reminds me of a girlfriend I had once. At a party, I went outside to take a piss. She saw it later, where my name was written in the snow. She left me."

"Well that seems extreme," Fallon said.

"Not really," he said. "It wasn't in my handwriting."

She punched him in the arm.

"Got you," Teffinger said.

She rolled her eyes and said, "Look at you, all proud of yourself."

"Yes I am."

The caveman taxi driver, Anton Fornier, emerged from the apartment building five minutes after he entered. As they followed, Teffinger said, "That was quick. We need to get a list of the tenants in that building."

Fallon agreed, then laughed.

"What?" Teffinger asked.

"Not your handwriting."

They spent the night on the houseboat, with Fallon down below in the stateroom with a gun by her side, and Teffinger under a black tarp between two storage units on the bow.

Listening.

Waiting.

Ready to pounce.

Ready to catch the killer once and for all.

Alive if possible.

His thoughts wandered. Tracy White was dead because of him. He could have captured the guy last night but didn't, meaning Michelle Berri might end up being yet another victim of his incompetence. Should he move to Paris? Should he derail this whole stupid plan of setting Fallon up as bait? He needed to call Sydney Heatherwood, to hear her voice again and make sure she was okay, and tell her about Fallon. He needed to call the Carr-Border gallery and see if his landscapes were selling. Even more so, he needed to set a blank canvas on an easel and get the smell of turpentine in his nose. He was thirty-four; would he ever have kids?

Sleep.

Sleep.

He needed sleep.

So badly.

As of two in the morning, no one had shown up yet to kill Fallon.

Teffinger closed his eyes just to rest them for a few seconds.

38

Day Five—July 16
Friday Morning

———————

When Deja woke before sunrise, Alexandra wasn't in the hotel room. She showed up ten minutes later, looking stressed. "Where were you?"

"Talking with some people."

"Who?"

"Just some people."

"I thought we were in this together."

"We are, but there are still a few things you're better off not knowing."

"Like what?"

Alexandra ignored her, looked at her watch and said, "Let's go, we've got to catch a puddle jumper to Luxor." An hour later they were in a bumpy sky, strapped into a noisy two-prop deathtrap, following the Nile Valley south. The valley was basically one long continuous oasis, striking in its beauty.

Alexandra, it turned out, had a change of heart as to how to proceed. Instead of trying to retrace Remy's steps to figure out how he came up with a map, she wanted to take a long shot.

"Are you afraid of snakes?" Alexandra asked.

Yes.

"Heights?"

Yes.

"Small enclosures?"

Yes.

Alexandra chuckled.

"Then one of us is going to remember today for a long time."

"The Valley of the Kings is broken into two sections," she said, "the East Valley and the West Valley. The East Valley is the important one. Over sixty tombs have been discovered there over the centuries, including King Tut's, which was found in 1922. The West Valley, by contrast, was hardly ever used. Only one tomb has been discovered there."

Okay.

"As a result, the East Valley has been the subject of repeated exploration and mapping," Alexandra said. "In recent years, that's included ground-penetrating radar. On several different occasions, explorers have officially declared that all of the tombs have been discovered. And though they still keep being found, the frequency is less and less. In my opinion, the East Valley still has a few nuggets to be found, but not many."

"So how are we going to find something if all these explorers haven't been able to?"

Good question.

"Okay, let's drop back a couple of thousand years and put ourselves in the shoes of the rich guy who robbed the tomb that got discovered six months ago," Alexandra said. "If we get caught, we're going to be subjected to a horrible death. Plus they'll force us to reveal where we stashed everything. That means they'll take it back from our son's burial site, meaning he won't cross over into immortality. So, the incentive is extremely high to not be caught."

Agreed.

"I mean, extremely high."

Agreed again.

"The last thing we want to do is to get caught."

Deja rolled her eyes.

"I get it."

"You don't want to get caught, do you?"

No.

She didn't.

"Okay," Alexandra said. "So what do you do, to not get caught?"

Deja didn't know.

"Tell me," she said.

"No, you figure it out."

Their seats rattled and the props occasionally misfired. Vegetation and sugarcane fields hugged the denim-blue waters of the Nile below. Otherwise the topography was barren desert.

Uninhabitable.

Mean.

Unforgiving.

Dangerous.

"Okay, I have it," Deja said. "We kill all the men we used to break into the tomb so they can't talk."

Alexandra smiled.

"Of course we do that," Alexandra said. "But that's only the beginning. What else?"

"I don't know, tell me."

"Tell yourself."

Deja cocked her head. "You have a mean streak in you. Do you know that?"

She pondered it but didn't come up with anything. Then she did, maybe. "Okay," she said, "I think I got it."

"Go on."

"If they suspect us, and dig up the son and find the stuff, we're dead."

Right.

"So we need to be sure they don't find the son."

Right.

"So what we do is have a traditional burial plot where they would expect it to be," Deja said, "except we leave that one empty. Then we bury him somewhere else—somewhere they won't find him."

Alexandra smiled.

"Go on."

"But we wouldn't want to use anyone else to help dig the second site, partially because they might tell someone, but mostly so that they don't go back later and rob it," Deja said. "That means that we have to dig the second site ourselves with our own two hands."

Right.

Keep going.

"But that will be hard work," Deja said. "So we need to find something that's already dug, like a cave or something."

"Bingo."

"And it will need to be far away from the main areas of activity so that no one stumbles on it."

Double bingo.

"And since no one has stumbled on it yet in the East Valley where all the exploration and mapping has taken place, it must be in the West Valley, or possibly even west of that."

Triple bingo.

Alexandra gave her a high five and said, "Congratulations, you're now the official owner of an archeological mind."

From Luxor International Airport they took a cab into the city, ate a healthy lunch and bought supplies.

Backpacks.

Flashlights.

Water.

Rope.

Food.

Sunscreen.

Hats.

A folding shovel.

A snakebite kit.

And more.

Then they were ready.

39

Day Five—July 16
Friday Noon

———————

arcel Durand dragged his P.I. body out of bed shortly before noon on Friday and pointed his forgettable face outside to find a café table in the sun and load up with coffee and food. Last night had been a bust. He watched the houseboat for hours from the shadows across the river.

It never felt right so he didn't make a move.

Maybe tonight.

Maybe in a month.

Time would tell.

He couldn't shake the irony that of all the illegal things he had done over the years, the one thing he didn't do—namely, kill the boxer—might be the thing that brings him down.

The caffeine worked its way into his blood and the sunshine went to his brain.

He thumbed through the morning paper.

Then his phone rang and the voice of a woman came through. "I'd like to meet with you regarding a potential project, if you have time," she said.

He had time.

He had time indeed.

An hour later he knocked on the door of a nice house in the Luxembourg Quarter. A curvy brunette, still striking even in her forties, opened the door and let him in.

She was Emmanuelle Atwood.

"Anton Fornier said you could be trusted," she said. "Is that true?"

Durand cocked his head.

"Have you ever heard of me before Anton mentioned my name?"

No.

She hadn't.

"There are two reasons for that," he said. "One, I keep my client's secrets secret. And two, I even keep myself a secret. I'm not in the phone book and never have been. I work only through referrals and word of mouth. Whatever it is you tell me, and whatever it is that you want me to find out, all that stays entirely between you and me. I don't even talk to my plants about it. In return, I'm the priciest P.I. you'll ever meet. I work only on a cash basis paid upfront and I don't make any promises except that you'll get my best efforts."

"Which are considerable, I assume."

Durand nodded.

"In my totally unbiased and humble opinion, oui."

She lit a cigarette.

"If I hire you, I'll need to tell you about some delicate matters," she said. "I don't want anything written down. I don't want any notes that someone might stumble across in one or five or ten years. I don't want anything anywhere, except in your head."

Durand pulled a pencil out of his pocket and broke it in two.

"There," he said.

"Did Anton tell you why we want to hire a P.I.?"

"Yes."

"So you know what will happen next, if you can find the man we're looking for?"

Yes.

He did.

"So if you take the job, you'd almost be an accomplice," she said.

True.

"Which gives me all the more reason to be absolutely sure that whatever gets said between us stays between us."

The woman studied him.

"I'll need two referrals," she said.

Durand stood up.

"Then you're out of luck," he said. "Because I don't tell anyone who my clients are, ever. Nor do I contact them and ask if they'll talk to other people."

The woman tossed her hair.

"Sit down," she said. "That was the answer I was looking for. How much of a retainer do you need?"

He told her.

She disappeared into a back room, returned a minute later and handed him an envelope. He folded it in half and stuffed it in his back pocket without looking inside.

"Okay, here's what's going on," she said.

Then she told him a story about a Blue Moon escort who got suffocated by a mystery man.

Durand frowned during most of it and at the end said, "This

is going to be tough. You need to appreciate that upfront."

She stood up and escorted him to the door.

"You'll find him," she said. Then she wrote a phone number on a piece of paper, folded it into fourths, and handed it to him. "This will be good for a while. Use it only when you have to, and call from a payphone."

Durand stuffed it in his wallet.

Then he wrote his number on a piece of paper and left.

From Blue Moon, Durand went to Verdant Park, to see if the blond prostitute was there, the one who said she was twenty-five but looked forty.

She was and smiled as he walked towards her.

"You dyed your hair."

Durand shuffled his feet. "This is sort of weird," he said. "But I was wondering if you wanted to go out sometime, you know, maybe get dinner or something like that."

She studied him.

Durand could read her thoughts—she was figuring out if he was trying to get sex for free—so he said, "It would just be a date, nothing more. I won't put the moves on you or anything." She looked as if she'd heard that before. "I promise. We'd get some food, take a walk, something simple like that. Get to know each other a little."

She exhaled and asked if he had a number.

He did and wrote it down.

She took it and said, "I'll think about it."

"Okay, great."

He turned and walked away.

She wouldn't call.

He already knew that because she never asked his name.

40

Friday morning, Teffinger stayed hidden in the house-boat while Fallon headed to the office, just in case the killer was waiting to see if a man emerged. In the lower quarters, he did pushups, crunches, squats and jumping jacks until his body ached. Then he showered and took a cab to the victims' house. He stretched out in Michelle Berri's bed and let the empty silence wash over him, to embed the reality that she was a flesh-and-blood human being and not just a case, a human being who was still missing.

He reflected on Tracy White.

The first time they met.

The way she smiled.

When he closed his eyes he could see her down at head-quarters sitting at a scratched wooden table, working with the sketch artist; and he could feel the beating of his heart as a clearer and clearer picture of the killer emerged.

Damn it.

That was such a long time ago.

He pulled the two pictures out of his shirt pocket, the pictures of the first victim, Amanda Peterson, the 22-year-old waitress who got her eyes gouged out, a green-eyed beauty brutally cut down before her life even started.

How did the killer choose her?

Did he see her on the street?

Did he bump into her at a club?

Something like Rex?

Teffinger grunted. He had asked these questions a hundred times, no, a thousand. He never gave himself an answer. Why did he keep asking the same stupid things over and over? He needed fresh questions.

He called Dr. Leigh Sandt, the FBI profiler from Quantico, Virginia. She actually answered and the sound of her voice made Teffinger pull up the image of a classy woman, about fifty, with fitness-club legs—the kind of legs men kill for, Tina Turner legs.

"It's me," he said.

"Nick?"

"Yes."

"Where are you—still in Paris?"

"Yes."

"That means some poor French woman is getting her feet pointed at the ceiling by an American," she said. "So what's the latest victim's name?"

Teffinger chuckled.

"Fallon."

Fallon?

Right.

"She sounds yummy," Leigh said.

Fallon.

"She's half the reason I called," Teffinger said. "I'm thinking about staying in Paris. Maybe join the CIA, if they have an office here. Do you have any connections?"

Silence.

"You wouldn't be happy in that group," she said. "Don't get too enamored with Paris. Living somewhere isn't about the buildings, it's about the people. The people who make up your life are all in Denver."

"Not all of them."

"Slow down and think about it Nick, that's all I'm saying."

"She's hot, did I mention that?"

"Put the little guy away and think it through."

"The little guy?"

"You know what I mean."

Then he told her the other half of the reason he called. He wanted to know if she had any way of finding out whether other women around the world outside the United States or Europe—say Japan or Australia or Thailand—got their eyes gouged out and reinserted backwards.

A pause.

"That would be a huge project," she said, "and it would take a truckload of time. If you're looking for another case to cross-reference in the hopes of finding a common denominator, you won't get it in time to help the missing woman—what's her name?"

"Michelle Berri."

"Right, her."

"Okay."

"Sorry," she said.

"No, that's fine. It's what I expected. I just got tired of asking myself the same questions over and over and needed a new one—that, and I wanted to hear the sound of your voice, but don't ever tell anyone because I'll deny it."

When he got to Fallon's office, she was at her desk with her shoes off, flicking a lighter and working the computer. A couple of papers with names sat in front of her. "We got a list of the tenants," she said, referring to the apartment building where the caveman taxi driver led them yesterday after leaving Blue Moon. "I'm running background checks on them as we speak."

Teffinger took a sip of coffee.

"That's a long shot," he said.

"I'll take a short shot, if you have one."

He didn't.

He wished he did, but he didn't.

A file sat on the corner of Fallon's desk.

"What's that?" he asked.

It was the file on Sharla DePaglia, the Blue Moon escort who got smothered.

"That's been there since Monday," Teffinger said. "How did you know that Blue Moon was somehow connected to the caveman?"

"A caveman," she said, "who may or may not be the caveman. But to answer your question, that file's never left my desk."

"I thought you said that woman—what's her name?"

"Sharla DePaglia."

"Right, her, I thought you said she got killed more than a year ago."

She nodded.

"Cold cases are like plants," she said. "They need to stay in the light, otherwise they die."

Teffinger understood.

He also understood that if he used that approach, he wouldn't have a desk left to work on.

"Mind if I take a look?"

"Knock yourself out."

41

Day Five—July 16
Friday Afternoon

———————————

The Valley of the Kings lies just west of Luxor, not far on the other side of the Nile greenbelt, in the barren and dangerous valley of the Theban hills. For nearly 500 years, from the 16th to the 11th centuries BC, kings and powerful nobles of the New Kingdom chose the valley as their final resting place. The thinking was that the remoteness of the location, together with the craggy cliffs, provided a natural protection from intruders and robbers.

More than sixty tombs had been located in the East Valley over time.

That compared to only one in the West Valley.

Deja and Alexandra took a cab as far into the valley as the roads allowed and then walked west. Right now, midday in July, the sun ruled the world and spit fiery air at every living thing it could find.

Tourists were minimal.

Movement was scarce.

All the sane people in the world were somewhere else.

Alexandra pointed and said, "That's the new tomb, the one we're trying to find the treasure of." Deja thought it would look like a pyramid. Instead, it was something more in the nature of a series of chambers that had been buried underground by the last three thousand years.

They passed through the valley and walked west on a lifeless camel trail wearing backpacks, floppy hats and sunglasses.

"Keep an eye out for snakes," Alexandra said. "They blend in so you have to make an effort to look for them."

Right.

Absolutely.

"They really get pissed if you step on them," Alexandra added.

Deja knew it was a joke and she should laugh but she couldn't because the heat had her in a stranglehold. "Maybe we should go back and wait until the sun goes down," she said.

"No time," Alexandra said. "If you start to feel faint or dizzy or weak or nauseous, let me know right away—or a headache."

"I'm fine, but just for the record, this is really hot."

"We just need to stay hydrated and go slow. I've been roaming this area since I was eight and, according to most reports, I'm still alive."

"Eight?"

"My parents brought me here more times than I can remember," Alexandra said. "They're the reason we're here right now."

"I don't follow."

"You will," she said. "Look over your shoulder every now and then. Be sure no one's on our tail."

Deja twisted her body around and scouted the desolate

landscape.

She saw no one and said so.

"Good."

Craggy cliffs jutted up on their immediate left as well as several hundred meters to their right. A kilometer later, the camel path ended.

They kept going west, into death's hands.

"Stay with me," Alexandra said. "Don't fall behind and don't get separated."

"I'm here."

Twenty steps later, Deja's foot came down on something; something softer than a rock.

She looked down and found herself standing on the head of a snake, a large snake.

She froze.

The reptile thrashed its body wildly from side to side.

"Don't move!" Alexandra said. "That's a viper!"

42

Day Five—July 16
Friday Afternoon

———————————

Prarie Canelle was a waitress at the Laughing Hat Cafe down the street from Durand's apartment. With a pale gothic face hidden behind thick black glasses, an ever-present pulled-back-tight ponytail, and a short 25-year-old frame with a round belly, no one ever accused her of being stunning.

Even Durand, as plain vanilla as he was, never paid her much attention.

But today, when he stopped in for a bite, she took his order with a shy smile and said, "I like what you did with your hair."

He looked at her.

Not at her glasses, as usual, but through her glasses into her eyes, where he saw something he never had before. He surprised himself by saying, "Would you like to get together sometime, when you're not working?"

She diverted her eyes, then threw him a sideways glance.

"I'm serious," Durand said.

"Well, if you really mean it, okay," she said.

"Good," Durand said. "Are you free tonight?"

She was.

"Great."

They made arrangements.

Then Durand headed home, sat on the terrace and listened to the street noises as he thought about the case for his newest client, Emmanuelle.

Emmanuelle of Blue Moon.

The story she told was simple but brutal. Emmanuelle was in a Rome nightclub called Neo a year ago, searching for new talent, when she spotted an incredibly exotic woman—a woman who was hunting other women, searching for forbidden night pleasures, kissing strangers as if she owned them, tasting their tongues and feeling their bodies.

She finally found one she liked, took her to the dance floor and melted with her. Emmanuelle got wet just watching them. Later, she went up and made a pitch.

Come to Paris.

Make truckloads of money.

The woman took Emmanuelle's number, kissed her on the lips and said, "Ciao."

But she called the next day and came to Paris two days later.

Her name was Sharla DePaglia.

On a Saturday night, a cabbie knocked on the door of Blue Moon, handed Emmanuelle an envelope, and left. Inside was cash—8,000 euros—and a piece of paper with a telephone number and a name.

Franco.

Emmanuelle dialed the number.

A man answered and said he was from Amsterdam.

He was referred to Blue Moon by a friend of his.

He was in Paris for the weekend.

He wanted a woman for a couple of hours, a kinky woman. Tonight.

"What are you going to do to her?" Emmanuelle asked.

"Tie her up, tease her, vibrate her to the point of orgasm but deny her, over and over, until she promises to give me the best blowjob of my life," he said.

"So you're not talking about whipping or spanking or pain?"

The man grunted.

"I'm perverted but I'm not sick."

"Where do you want this to happen."

He told her.

A building was being renovated.

They'd have privacy there.

Silence.

"I'll call you back in a few minutes," Emmanuelle said.

Then she dialed Sharla DePaglia, who answered with cocaine in her voice and club noise in the background. Emmanuelle explained the gig and Sharla said she'd take it.

Emmanuelle called Franco back and said it was a go.

A woman would show up in thirty minutes.

"Since this Marco guy didn't have any history with us, I sent a man named Jean-Pierre over a half hour after Sharla was supposed to get there, just to make sure everything was okay. The doors were locked and the windows were boarded up, but he found a crack big enough to peek through. What he saw he could hardly believe. There were two women there, not just one. They were both tied in a standing spread-eagle position, facing each other, stomach to stomach. One of the women had a plastic bag duct-taped over her head and was thrashing around like crazy. When Jean-Pierre saw that, he kicked the window in. By the time he got there, though, Sharla was dead and the man was gone."

"Did he get a look at the man?"

"No."

"No?"

"No, unfortunately—the man had his back to him the whole time," Emmanuelle said. "Anyway, Jean-Pierre cut the other woman down and then they got the hell out of there."

"And this other woman, who was she?"

"She turned out to be someone from London, England who Sharla picked up in the club that night," Emmanuelle said. "They were together when I called. She just went along with Sharla for the ride."

"What's her name?"

Emmanuelle cocked her head.

"She was terrified after this happened," Emmanuelle said. "She made me promise I'd keep her out of it and I intend to keep that promise. But she got a good look at the man. If you find him, she's willing to come to Paris and confirm whether it's him or not."

Durand nodded.

"Good."

"That way I'll be positive I'm not having the wrong man killed," Emmanuelle said.

Durand retreated in thought.

Was there anything else he needed to know at this point?

Yes.

There was.

"Do you still have the piece of paper with the phone number that came in the envelope?"

No.

She threw it away.

"We traced the number, though, early on," she said. "It was a public phone."

"Where?"

"Near the Eiffel Tower."

Durand grunted.

"Sneaky little bastard, isn't he?"

Yes.

He is.

"And I want him to be a dead sneaky little bastard," she said. "So do your job well."

"How's he going to die?"

"The same way he dished it out, except over and over."

"Does Fornier know that?"

"No, but he won't have a problem with it."

43

Day Five—July 16
Friday Morning

Teffinger closed the Sharla DePaglia file, set it back on the corner of Fallon's desk and said, "I don't think the killer let the other woman go on purpose. I think he got interrupted in progress. She intrigued him more than Sharla did. He wanted to have special time with her by letting her watch Sharla die. That increased her terror and correspondingly increased the tingle in his cock."

Fallon took a sip of coffee.

"You're such a poet."

Teffinger nodded.

"It doesn't come easy, I have to work at it."

She flicked a lighter.

"So who interrupted them?"

"Probably someone from Blue Moon," Teffinger said. "If it had been a construction worker, coming back to get tools he forgot or whatever, he would have stuck around to tell everyone what a hero he was. The big question is whether the person who interrupted everything got a look at the killer or not."

"It doesn't matter," Fallon said.

"Why not?"

"Because Blue Moon is a dead end," she said. "They're not cooperating."

"That's because you haven't persuaded them to."

"Meaning what?"

"Meaning they talk or you drive their clients away," Teffinger said. "Hit them in the wallet."

"You mean purse," Fallon said.

Teffinger nodded.

Right.

Purse.

"I'm impressed," Fallon said. "That's a good project for a month from now. But right now I want to concentrate on our caveman taxi driver."

"Who is somehow connected to Blue Moon."

"Maybe," Fallon said. "But if your point is that we should divert our attention to a cold case in hopes that it will throw light on a current one, then I think we're going too far off course. The connection is too indirect to justify suddenly throwing all our time at Blue Moon."

Teffinger shrugged.

"All I'm saying is, it takes a certain kind of person to suffocate someone, and it also takes a certain kind of person to gouge someone's eyes out. It wouldn't surprise me a bit if both those persons turned out to be the same person."

"Maybe yes, maybe no."

The background checks on the apartment tenants didn't produce much of interest, other than the fact that two of them turned out to be prostitutes.

Grade C.

Not Blue Moon material.

Whoever the caveman went to see yesterday after he left Blue Moon was a mystery.

"Now what?"

Teffinger shrugged.

"We'll follow him tonight and see if he ends up staking out the bait, namely your houseboat."

Suddenly a figure appeared in the office doorway—Targaux. "Something unpleasant just happened," he said. "Tourists from all over the world came to see our fair city and paid hard-earned money to see it from one of the best vantage points we have, namely from the sunny decks of one of our tour boats. The problem is, as they cruised down the Seine under a perfect Paris sky, they ended up seeing something that wasn't exactly on the tour guide's itinerary."

Fallon knew where this was heading and winced.

"A floater?"

Targaux nodded.

"Since you love that floater smell so much, I thought I'd let you have the honors."

"You are pure evil."

"Thank you."

"You're going to hell someday," Fallon said. "You know that, I hope."

He nodded.

"And it will be a worse place when you get there," she added.

Targaux laughed, then got serious.

"Be discrete. This is down by the Eiffel Tower." He looked at Teffinger and said something in French.

"What'd he say?" Teffinger said.

"He said, Keep her out of trouble." She gave him a sideways look. "It just goes to show he doesn't know you that well. Because if he knew you, he would have said that to me about you."

44

Day Five—July 16
Friday Afternoon

A s the viper thrashed its body wildly from side to side under Deja's foot, Alexandra ripped her backpack off and got down on all fours behind the reptile. She tried to catch it by the tail, but couldn't. Then she finally got a grip on it and stretched it out. "When I count to three, lift your foot up."

"You mean on three?"

"Right, as in one … two … foot up."

"Okay."

"Ready?"

"Yes."

"Okay, here we go."

One—

Two—

Three!

Deja lifted her foot as Alexandra simultaneously flung the snake with all her might. The reptile twisted in the air as it soared and landed with a thud six steps away. A tiny cloud of dust kicked up. The reptile curled up and made a terrible sound, something in the nature of a rolling FFFFFFFFFF—

Then it slithered at them with amazing speed.

They ran and didn't stop for fifty steps.

When they turned around, it was nowhere in sight.

Alexandra exhaled and said, "See, I told you they get mad if you step on them."

Deja knew it was a joke and should laugh but all she could do was say, "It tried to bite you, when you flung it. Did you see it?"

"No."

"It snapped its fangs when it flew past your face," Deja said.

Alexandra fixated on something behind them. Deja turned to see a man, far behind, but close enough to tell he was watching through binoculars.

"Who the hell is that?"

Silence.

"There's no way the looters could have followed us here," Deja said. "Not all the way from Paris."

Probably not.

But if not, who was it?

"My guess is it's one of the locals," Alexandra said. "Everyone around here knows about the missing treasure. When they see someone like you and me walking around, it's worth the time to follow us, just in case we're archeologists who know something they don't."

"Meaning if we find the treasure, they take it."

Alexandra nodded.

"We need to abort," she said.

Deja wiped sweat off her forehead with the back of her hand.

The sun beat down relentlessly.

She could still feel the viper's head under her foot.

"So all this was for nothing?"

Alexandra nodded.

"It was for right now," she said. "We're going to have to come back after dark."

They turned around and headed back. The man with the binoculars disappeared and they never saw him again. Alexandra said, "a weird thought—maybe he's not a local after all. Just out of curiosity, who knows that you came to Egypt?"

No one.

"You didn't tell anyone?"

No.

She didn't.

Well, wait a minute.

That wasn't exactly true.

She did tell one person.

"Who's that?"

Her boss at the law firm.

A man named Yves Petit.

"But I told him not to tell anyone and he said he wouldn't," Deja said.

"Yves Petit, huh?"

Deja grunted.

"He's not involved in anything, if that's what you're getting at."

"How do you know?"

"Because he isn't, that's how."

Silence.

"Didn't you say before that the guy who hired the P.I. was a client of the law firm?" Alexandra asked.

Right.

He was.

A man named Nicholas Ringer.

He lives in Nice.

He owns a shipyard.

Ringer Yachts.

"Do Yves Petit and Nicholas Ringer know each other?"

Deja nodded.

"Yves is Ringer's attorney," she said. "Why? What are you getting at?"

"I don't know," Alexandra said. "I'm seeing something, but it's too vague to know what."

Ten minutes later, Alexandra said, "Maybe Yves Petit put Nicholas Ringer up to hiring the P.I., as a way to keep track of you and, by association, me. And by double association, the treasure. Maybe the guy with the binoculars is Yves Petit's eyes."

Deja laughed.

"Everything's a conspiracy with you. Why is that?"

"Because in this business, everything is a conspiracy, darling."

Deja wasn't impressed.

"Yves would never be involved in anything," she said. "I mean, the man's getting me into law school, and I didn't even ask him. That's the kind of person he is."

Well, that's weird.

"Tell me about that," Alexandra said.

Deja did.

And when she finished, Alexandra said, "Maybe he did that so you'll be indebted to him. That way you end up talking to him more. You end up telling him things that you might not otherwise."

That's nuts.

"You already told him about me and our treasure hunt, right? Or, if not him directly, you told Nicholas Ringer, who obviously talks to him. Yves Petit has a direct line into everything that's going on."

Deja was about to protest but didn't and instead thought about it as they walked.

"You're thinking about it," Alexandra said.

True.

She was.

"But that doesn't mean you're right," Deja said.

"It doesn't mean I'm wrong, either," Alexandra said. "Tell me about Yves Petit. Who is he, deep down? What else don't I know?"

45

Durand got a call from his client who said to look on page 5 of Tuesday's paper, because the man pictured there bore a striking resemblance to the man in the sketch that Durand faxed over—the sketch of the man who killed Luc Trickett, the boxer, while Durand hid behind a door upstairs.

Durand ran down a copy of the paper.

His first reaction, when he saw the picture, was that the guy did indeed have a resemblance to the man who shot the boxer. His second reaction was that the guy looked even more like Anton Fornier.

The caveman.

The taxi driver.

The hitman.

He read the story. The man was a suspect in the murder of someone named Tracy White and the disappearance of her roommate, Michelle Berri.

Interesting.

Anton was the kind of guy who could do something like that all day long.

Is it possible that Anton was actually the man Durand saw through the crack in the door at the boxer's house, but he didn't recognize him at the time?

The more he thought about it, the more it made sense.

The man Durand saw that night had seemed familiar in some intangible way. Anton always had a beard, so Durand wouldn't have recognized him with it gone. The boxer's death was clearly a hit, and Anton was a hitman. Anton was the right size.

Interesting.

Disturbing, too.

Durand always pictured finding out who the man was who killed the boxer and then anonymously giving the information to the police, if the need arose—which it likely would, since the cops had a witness placing Durand at the murder scene. But now, for that plan to work, Durand would have to give up Anton—a friend; a friend who had just landed him a very lucrative assignment for Blue Moon to be precise.

Durand exhaled.

Nothing was ever easy.

Nothing.

Ever.

46

Day Five—July 16
Friday Afternoon

The floater was missing one head and two hands—they'd been sawed off. A large section of flesh was missing from his left arm. He'd been shot in the upper chest.

"He's definitely dead," Teffinger said.

Fallon studied the arm wound.

"That's not from a prop," she said.

"Want me to tell you what it's from?" Teffinger asked.

"Yeah, tell me."

"What do I get if I do?"

"I don't know. What do you want?"

"You."

"You already have me," she said, "unless you're talking about me being your sex slave or something like that."

Teffinger cocked his head.

"I hadn't thought about it in terms like that," he said. "But that sounds reasonable."

She chuckled.

"Okay, you have a deal," she said. "Now tell me."

"No reneging," he said.

"I won't."

"Tonight," he said.

"Whenever you want. Now tell me."

"You'll notice that this particular person is missing a head and two hands," Teffinger said.

Right.

She noticed.

"That's so he can't be identified," Teffinger said. "The wound to the arm is there for the same reason. He had a tattoo there, a tattoo that got cut off and thrown away."

She smiled.

"So what are you going to do to your little sex slave, now that you have one?"

"I'm not sure yet," he said. "What are my limits?"

None.

Not a one.

"You can even invite your little friend Sophia if you want."

"Yeah?"

"Sure."

They worked up a general idea of the floater's height, weight and age, and compared that to missing person reports.

Negative.

Then there wasn't much more they could do without knowing who he was. Maybe his head would show up tomorrow, although they doubted it. It probably got buried somewhere or bagged up and thrown in a dumpster.

"I have a confession to make," Fallon said.

"What?"

"I already figured out the tattoo thing before you told me," she said. Teffinger must have had a look on his face because she added, "Don't worry, you still won."

"Good, I'm already making plans."

"You're so evil."

47

Day Five—July 16
Friday Evening

———————

At sunset Friday evening, Deja and Alexandra armed themselves with a bottle of wine and hiked down to the Nile where the air was cool and the water was magic. Deja always pictured it as muddy brown and filled with sharp yellow teeth looking for something to chomp on. In reality, it was blue and beautiful and, according to Alexandra, relatively safe in this stretch.

They didn't bring glasses and passed the bottle.

The alcohol dropped warm and tingly into their stomachs.

Everything softened.

Deja didn't have to ask what the plan was for tomorrow. They had already talked about it three or four times The plan was that they'd sneak out of the hotel tomorrow morning while it was still dark outside and get to where they were today by the crack of dawn. In other words, they'd walk the whole way they did today, except in the dark.

"Got a question," Deja said. "How do we see the snakes?"

"We won't need to," Alexandra said.

"Why not?"

"Because they'll see us."

"Not funny," Deja said.

"A little funny," Alexandra said. "Hey, I just thought of something, speaking of snakes—two to one."

Two to one?

What did that mean?

"That's the score now," she said. "I'm going to count that snake thing this afternoon as a save. Now you've saved me twice and I've saved you once."

"You still owe me one," Deja said.

"Don't worry, I'll have plenty of chances to even the score. Maybe tomorrow."

Enough chitchat.

Was the treasure really there?

Was all this brain damage and body damage worth it?

So far, Alexandra had kept the details sketchy, but now told Deja more. Alexandra was with her parents, eighteen years ago when she was ten, west of the West Valley. At that time, the East Valley was being explored to death because that's where all the tombs were being found. Alexandra's parents were the only archeologists straying so far to the west, off the beaten path, way off the beaten path, stupidly way off the beaten path according to everyone who had half a brain.

One day her father—Victor Reed—spotted something strange on the face of a craggy cliff, a considerable ways above the valley floor, twenty meters or more.

It looked like a small opening, possibly the mouth of a cave.

It also looked like someone had tried to hide it by filling the opening with rocks. Because it was wedged into the cliff, between outcroppings on each side, it wasn't visible from an angle. The only way to see it was to be directly in front of it, look up at that exact moment, and then be alert enough to detect the slight variation in texture between the cliff itself and the smaller rocks that filled the opening, assuming it was an opening because it might also be nothing more than a ledge where falling rocks accumulated.

"Anyway," Alexandra said, "it was interesting enough that dad wanted to climb up and take a look. He got a third of the way up and got bitten by a viper."

"You're kidding," Deja said.

No she wasn't.

The area was full of them, even then.

"My mom treated him as good as she could at the scene, then we climbed on the camels and headed back to civilization to get proper medical treatment," Alexandra said. "He turned out to be fine, with no permanent damage. Unfortunately though, we never ended up back at that particular part of the universe again."

"So you haven't been back there in eighteen years?"

"Correct."

"Do you remember where it was? I mean, you were only ten—"

Alexandra nodded.

"I was already an archeologist," she said. "A baby one, admittedly, but even then I used to make mental maps of where I was, based on vantage points, rock formations and things like that."

Interesting.

"Where we turned around today, that was about a half kilometer short of where we were going."

"So we were almost there."

Yes.

Almost.

Deja frowned.

"It seems to me that even if it turns out to be a cave, it's too high up and is too inaccessible. Remember, our theory is that the father took everything there by himself. Maybe he piled everything on a camel or two and made the trip by moonlight. But, even then, how would he get everything up the cliff? Especially a coffin—"

Alexandra chuckled.

"Remember, this happened more than three thousand years ago," she said. "The cave might very well have been on or very close to the valley floor at that time." She stood up. "Come on, let's get some sleep. Tomorrow we either find the treasure or go back to Cairo and try to trace Remy's footsteps."

Deja muscled to her feet.

"Snakes," she said. "It's almost like they're guarding the place."

48

Day Five—July 16
Friday Night

Prarie the waitress lived in a tiny apartment within walking distance of the Laughing Hat Cafe. Durand knocked on her door at eight Friday night with a pounding heart, still not sure where to take her. He had money and she didn't, that was the problem. If he treated her like a queen, he wouldn't be sure if she liked him for him or for the good times. On the other hand, he wanted to be someone special to her, which meant someone who didn't ply her with cheap wine at a dive bar and then slip a hand between her thighs.

She opened the door.

The usual ponytail was gone.

In its place were thick flowing locks.

Behind black glasses, plain eyes now had makeup.

Plain lips were now sultry pink.

The usual tattered jeans had turned into a short white dress.

Her legs were nice, nicer than most in fact.

"I'm in love," Durand said.

She diverted her eyes.

"I'm glad you came," she said. "I didn't know if you would."

Durand smelled wine on her breath and said, "Of course I would."

"I know that now."

"So what do you want to do?"

She didn't care.

Whatever he wanted.

Durand took her to a five-star restaurant on Champs-Elysees and spent more money than she made in a week. From there they went to a high-society bar two doors down and drank exotic drinks until the giggles came. Then they walked down the boulevard, soaking in the Arc de Triomphe, the traffic, the bright lights and the Parisian buzz with their arms around each other.

Drunk.

Groping.

Alive.

They ended up by the Seine.

Prarie reached under her dress, pulled white cotton panties off and twirled them on her finger in front of Durand's face. Then she threw them into the river.

"You don't have to do this," he said.

"I want to."

"You sure?"

She scouted around, then took his hand and led him to the darkest place she could find. And there, on the shadowy banks of the Seine under a perfect Paris night, Durand's life changed.

Just like that.

49

Day Six—July 17
Saturday Morning

———————

L ast night turned out to be a great big, dinosaur-sized waste of time. Teffinger and Fallon watched the houseboat from the shadows across the river. No one came to stake it out, no one walked past it suspiciously and cast an evil eye in the windows. At one in the morning they gave up, climbed aboard, stuffed the blankets of the main bed with cushions—just in case—and went to sleep in the aft cabin.

Nothing weird happened.

No gunfire shattered the windows.

No firebombs landed on deck.

That was last night.

Now it was morning.

They slept until nine, jogged and showered. The first pot of coffee was almost gone when Fallon's phone rang. Teffinger studied the curves of her body as she talked in French and stuck her tongue out at him. She hung up, looked at him and said, "You feel like going to see a head?"

He shrugged.

"Whose?"

"Mr. Floater's."

"How do you know it's his?"

"Because it's not attached to anything," she said.

Forty-five minutes later, they pulled up behind several police cars parked on a country road south of Paris. The head had been found in a black plastic bag, fifteen meters off the road, where someone had thrown it into the woods. It got discovered by a man who stopped to water a tree and then wandered over to see what the stench was all about.

The crime unit was already there.

Photographing.

Processing.

They were the same guys who fished the body out yesterday.

The head was still lying on the ground, eerily staring at the sun with open eyes through a rip in the plastic. Fallon moved a flap with a twig to get a better look. A mean pot-marked face with a chipped tooth came into fuller view.

"Cute," she said.

"Recognize him?" Teffinger asked.

"Yeah. He looks like you before your first pot of coffee."

While she talked with the crime unit in French, Teffinger walked up the road for a couple hundred meters, then returned and walked in the other direction. Fifty steps later he came to what he thought he might.

He got Fallon and brought her over, not telling her why.

Then he pointed to a second plastic bag in the brush, fifteen meters off the road, a bag with a foul stench. "If you want to shake the guy's hand for giving you job security, I'm guessing that you can reach inside that bag and do it."

She looked at him, shocked, and said, "Damn you're good."

He chuckled.

"Leave my sexual abilities out of this. We're at work."

She punched him on the arm.

"You need to be professional," he added. "Stay focused on the scene." Then he got serious. "There are at least two people involved. Someone was driving and someone else was flinging the bags. The flinger was a man, given the distance. Either a man or a woman could have been driving." A pause. "Or a donkey or a midget, which reminds me of a dream I had last night—"

She rolled her eyes.

"I'm not sure I can spend the whole day with you."

"People tell me it's not easy," he said.

By mid-afternoon they had the head and hands identified as belonging to a man named Pascal Lambert, who lived in a run-down house south of the city, not more than five kilometers from where his head got tossed.

They parked on the street and slipped gloves on as they walked up a weed-invested drive.

"Remember, don't step on the rats," Teffinger said.

Fallon smiled.

"Or ride them."

Inside, thirty minutes later, they found something interesting.

Very interesting.

50

Day Six—July 17
Saturday Morning

True to plan, Deja and Alexandra woke up three hours before daybreak, got dressed without turning the lights on, snuck out the rear exit, and walked west into the Egyptian nightscape with the moon as their flashlight.

The rocks radiated heat even now, but were nothing compared to yesterday.

"It feels like a glacier storm," Deja said. "I can actually drink water and it doesn't run straight out my pores."

Alexandra chuckled.

"You're turning into a camel," she said. "By this time tomorrow you'll have a hump."

"Can't wait."

"You'd look good in a hump, actually."

"You think?"

"No question," Alexandra said. "Not everyone can pull them off. But a few can. Quasimodo, for example."

True.

"And that lab assistant from Young Frankenstein—what

was his name?"

"Igor."

Right.

Igor.

"He could wear a hump with the best of them," Alexandra said. "And now you."

They made good time and got to the general area a half hour before daybreak. That gave them a chance to sit down, eat and drink. As the landscape lost its black edge, they hid behind an outcropping and studied the topography through binoculars.

They saw no one.

When it got light enough, they went to where the cave should be.

It wasn't there.

Alexandra studied the landscape again, harder, and pointed.

"It should be right there," she said, "wedged between those two outcroppings. We should be able to see it from right where we're standing."

"There's nothing there," Deja said.

Alexandra paced.

"Something's wrong," she said.

She spotted a sand viper thirty steps away and threw a rock at it—missing by three meters. The reptile froze, not knowing what happened or what direction it came from. Alexandra threw again, landing within a meter. This time the snake darted away.

"All I can figure is that small stones dribbled down the cliff over the last eighteen years and covered it up even more. I need to get up there and poke around. You stay down here and keep watch."

Okay.

Fine.

Alexandra took everything out of her backpack except a folding shovel, flashlight, rope and water. Then she climbed.

The crag was steep and dangerous.

"Be careful," Deja said.

"Don't worry."

Halfway up, Alexandra lost her footing and almost fell. Then she stayed there, right where she was, until she got her nerve back.

She climbed even higher, twice as high—twenty meters.

"It should be right about here," she shouted.

"Do you see anything?"

"No, but the rocks look loose."

She wedged herself into a crag as best she could and clawed at the rocks with her hand. She was right. They were loose and broke away with little effort. She worked harder, removing an outer layer of smaller rocks and dirt. Below that, she found larger rocks that looked like they had been set in place.

"This is it!" she said.

Deja was about to say, "Great," when something on the ground caught her peripheral vision. She focused on it.

A snake!

I was huge, not more than three meters away, coming right at her and making a terrible attack sound.

Suddenly a scream came from above—a bloodcurdling scream, so loud and desperate that Deja took her eyes off the reptile and looked up.

What she saw she could hardly believe.

Alexandra was falling, out of control.

51

Day Six—July 17
Saturday Morning

Durand woke Saturday morning to find Prarie sleeping next to him, nude, on her stomach, breathing heavily. He muscled up, detected a slight but not overly-fierce hangover, and admired the curvature of her body as he walked to the shower. Her ass was round. So was her belly but, like the rest of her body, it was also firm.

Her skin was soft, taut and flawless.

Her purse and glasses were on the dresser.

Her dress, bra and shoes were in a drunken pile on the floor next to the bed.

She wore no panties.

They were in the Seine somewhere.

He was glad she was here and after he showered, he made her coffee and breakfast to prove it. Then he walked her back to her apartment, arm in arm under a nice Paris sky, while they made plans for tonight.

On the walk back to his apartment, Durand's client called and asked, "Anything new?"

"I'm not sure yet," Durand said. "The caveman on page 5 of the paper—who may or may not be the same man I saw from behind the bedroom door—has a striking resemblance to a taxi driver."

"Who?"

Durand almost said, Anton Fornier, but didn't. "I'd rather not throw names around until I dig into it further."

"When will that be?"

Soon.

Today.

"I still don't get your interest in all this," Durand said.

"Just keep working," the client said. "Do you need more money?"

No.

The money was fine.

Plenty left.

Late morning, Durand went to the Laughing Hat Cafe, took a sidewalk table in the sun, and drank coffee while Prarie hustled past and brushed up against him as often as she could without arousing suspicion. Durand called some of his more discrete underground sources to find out what he could on Anton Fornier. They all told him the same thing—there were rumors that the man did hits on the side, but they didn't know if that was true or not.

Okay.

Thanks.

Then someone told him something he didn't know.

Fornier had a brother in Cairo.

Serge Fornier.

A man who looked even more like a caveman than Anton,

if you can believe it.

Durand fired up his laptop, logged onto the net and found a number of articles on Serge Fornier, who turned out to be an archeologist. A few of those articles had a picture of the man who actually did look more like a caveman than Anton.

Interesting.

Durand cocked his head and studied the man's face.

Was he the one Durand saw from behind the door?

The one who killed Luc Trickett, the boxer?

Suddenly Prarie was at his table, topping off his coffee, filling his senses with the aroma of her perfume. "Is everything okay here, sir?"

He motioned for her to lean in.

She did.

He whispered in her ear, "Do you have any idea how hard it is to not sweep everything off this table and throw you on top of it?"

She diverted her eyes, then looked at him and said, "I'm pretty sure they have rules against that here. But I'll check with the manager, if you want."

Durand chuckled.

"Would you?"

52

Day Six—July 17
Saturday Afternoon

———————

At the floater's house under a beat-beyond-death couch in the living room, Teffinger spotted a piece of pizza that looked like it dated back to the caveman days. That's not what got his attention, though. What got his attention was the large manila envelope lying next to it. An envelope that looked like it had been inadvertently dropped and kicked. Fallon pulled it out, handling it only by the edges.

Inside were ten or twelve pages of handwritten notes in a foreign language.

"I'm pretty sure this is Egyptian writing," Fallon said.

Teffinger shrugged.

He didn't know.

He knew English, that was it.

Behind the notes were ten or so large color photographs of ancient documents inscribed with hieroglyphic writing.

Pascal Lambert, the floater, was a common thug.

A mercenary for hire.

A lowlife.

"Weird," Teffinger said. "These are the kinds of things an archeologist would have, not a scumbag like the floater."

Fallon frowned.

"I think I know where he got them," she said.

Really?

Where?

"From a man named Remy Lafayette, a dead man named Remy Lafayette to be precise, a dead man named Remy Lafayette who got murdered about two weeks ago by someone who stole a lot of his archeological files, to be even more precise," she said.

Teffinger raised an eyebrow.

"So your theory is that the floater killed this archeologist—"

"—Remy Lafayette—"

"—Right, him."

She nodded.

"I wish Remy Lafayette had been my case. I'd have one solved."

Teffinger raked his hair back with his fingers. It hung in place for a second and flopped back down over his forehead. "You'd have one half-solved," he said.

Half solved?

Meaning what?

"Meaning if you're right in that the floater killed this Remy guy, then it's pretty obvious who killed the floater."

He paused to let the words sink in and watched her face as she got a distant expression and processed the information.

Then she looked at him and said, "A co-conspirator."

Teffinger nodded.

"That would be my guess," he said. "The floater and someone else, maybe more than one someone else, killed the archeologist and took his papers. Then they had a falling out for whatever reason and the floater ended up floating. That's why they cut off his head and hands, so he couldn't be identified and couldn't tie them to the archeologist." Teffinger tilted his head. "The more I think about it, you only have it one-third solved, not a half. That's because two people were involved in throwing the floater's head out the window."

Fallon nodded.

Right.

The man who threw the bags.

And the driver.

"Who could have been a man or a woman or a donkey or a midget," Fallon said.

Teffinger nodded.

"Right."

Fallon called Targaux, who was personally handling the Remy Lafayette case given its high visibility, and filled him in. "You need to confirm that the papers we found belonged to your victim," she told him.

Silence.

"You got the lead, why don't you run with it? His niece might know, I'd start with her," Targaux said. "Hold on—let me pull the file." Papers rustled. "Okay, here it is, her name is Deja Lafayette. She's a linguist at a law firm called Berthrand, Roux and Blanc, in La Defense. Got a pencil?"

She did, and wrote down the information.

"You going to jump on it?" Targaux asked.

"I'm already off the ground."

"Let me know when you land," he said.

When Fallon hung up, Teffinger asked, "Why does that law

NIGHT WITNESS

firm sound familiar?"

"That's where that lawyer works."

Teffinger didn't follow and wrinkled his forehead to prove it.

What lawyer?

"The lawyer who wasn't the page 5 caveman," Fallon said.

Bingo.

Now he remembered.

"The guy who wasted our time," he said.

"No, the guy who saved our time," she said. "Come on, we have a dead archeologist's niece we need to talk to. Deja Lafayette."

53

Day Six—July 17
Saturday Morning

———————

D eja jumped at the exact moment the viper struck, but did it too slow and too late. The reptile's head hit her foot with a solid force, grabbed on for a second and then released her. She had been hit, no question. What she didn't know is whether the fangs had penetrated her shoe or not. The snake immediately curled up to strike again.

Alexandra fell directly on it and pinned half of its body under her.

The snake flailed its head wildly and then struck.

Again.

And again.

And again.

But each time it only got the backpack.

Deja picked up the closest rock she could find and brought it down on the reptile's head with as much force as she could, disorienting it but not killing it. Then she grabbed Alexandra's arm and pulled her off. The viper immediately headed away, twisting with disorientation, as if its eyes had been smashed.

Deja kicked dirt at it.

Alexandra didn't move or make a sound.

She was either unconscious or dead.

Deja tried to wake the woman but couldn't. Alexandra didn't respond to shaking or shouting or face slapping. On closer examination, she wasn't dead. Breath came from her mouth and blood pumped through her veins.

What to do?

If she left to get help, Alexandra would almost certainly get fangs sunk into her face. So instead, Deja poured water on the woman's hair, covered her face with a hat and then gave her shade by standing over her.

Time passed.

Then more.

Then something happened.

Alexandra moaned and muscled to a sitting position.

Then she made a painful sound, fell onto her back and held her left arm with her right hand.

"Are you okay?"

"No, my arm—"

From what they could tell, Alexandra's left arm was broken somewhere between the elbow and the wrist. "We need to get you to a doctor," Deja said.

"No."

No?

No.

"We need to keep going," Alexandra said. "This could be our only chance."

"Keep going? You can't climb with that arm, are you nuts?"

"I don't mean me, I mean you," Alexandra said. "You need

to get up there and get into that cave."

Deja pictured it and didn't like what she saw.

Her heart raced.

"I don't like heights," she said. "I already told you that."

"You'll be fine," Alexandra said. "Just go slow and watch your footing."

Deja shook her head.

"No, there's no way—"

"You have to," Alexandra said.

Deja kicked the dirt.

"Look," she said, "here's what we'll do. We'll go back to Luxor and get you to a doctor. Then I'll call Yves Petit, the lawyer in my firm. He'll either come down himself or send someone who can be trusted."

"No."

"Why not?"

"Because he's up to something," Alexandra said. "We already talked about that. The only people we can trust are each other." She scouted the horizon. "Hurry up, before someone starts wandering around out here and spots us."

54

Day Six—July 17
Saturday Afternoon

Durand knocked on Anton Fornier's door Saturday afternoon. No one answered, meaning the caveman was out driving his taxi somewhere like he was supposed to. Good. Durand worked the lock until it clicked, stepped inside and closed the door behind him. A gray cat trotted over and brushed against his leg.

Durand picked it up.

"What's your name?"

The cat didn't answer but it did purr.

"Friendly little guy, aren't you?"

He kept the cat in one arm and scouted around. The apartment was nice, way nicer than a taxi driver could afford. Anton was too obvious with his money. That would get him in trouble someday. The question right now, however, is whether the apartment held any evidence that either Anton or his even-more-caveman-like Cairo brother, Serge, killed Luc Trickett—the boxer.

The boxer's office had been ransacked.

So Durand concentrated on Anton's office, to see if anything belonging to the boxer was there. The boxer's laptop would be the most obvious thing.

He found nothing.

No laptop.

No papers with the boxer's name on them.

Nothing.

He did find a suitcase in the man's bedroom closet, which may or may not have been the one used to haul off the boxer's stuff.

A full-sized computer sat on a desk.

Durand fired it up, copied the files and shut it down.

Then he grabbed a banana out of a fruit bowl, stuck it in his pocket, gave the cat a pat on the head, made sure no nosy neighbors were in the hallway, and left.

No one saw him.

No one ever saw him.

He was invisible.

55

Day Six—July 17
Saturday Afternoon

_____

When they stepped outside the floater's rat-in-a-closet house, the sunshine hit Teffinger's face and went straight to his brain. Fallon walked next to him wearing that face, that body, that raw passion just behind her eyes. She tossed the mysterious Egyptian envelope into the back seat and fired up the engine.

Teffinger squeezed her leg, just above the knee, and said, "Go to the boat."

She looked over.

He expected her to ask, "Why?"

She didn't.

She knew why.

It was in his eyes.

They got to the boat, went below and closed the curtains. Fallon took a long swallow of wine from a bottle and passed it to Teffinger.

He drank, then set it down.

Fallon dropped to her knees, put her hands on top of her

head and said, "So what are you going to do with your little sex slave, now that you have me where you want me?"

Teffinger tilted his head.

He'd forgotten about that little bet down by the river.

Well, that wasn't quite true.

He'd only half forgotten about it.

"What do you want me to do?"

"Whatever you want."

"Whatever I want, huh?"

"Oui, whatever you want."

He walked around her.

Close.

Playing with her hair.

"Tie me up," she said.

"Be careful—"

"I want to be in your control," she said. "Your one hundred percent control." She stood up, pulled a black duffel bag out of a storage compartment and tossed it on the bed. "That's my bag of goodies. Find something you like."

He checked.

Inside were cuffs, rope, blindfolds, feathers, vibrators and other assorted toys. Then she showed him something else, namely eyehooks at the corners of the bed.

He tied her down, spread-eagle on her back, tight, wearing only a thong. She tried to wiggle her hips but could hardly move. He sat on the edge of the bed and ran a finger gently across her lips. "Looks like someone's stuck," he said.

"You're so evil."

He straddled her stomach and played with her nipples. Then he put his hands on her wrists and lightly ran his fingers down her arms.

Her body tensed.

Teffinger's fingers passed over her underarms and something happened he didn't expect.

She laughed.

She tried to stifle it but couldn't.

It was definitely a laugh.

"Well, it looks like someone's ticklish," he said.

"No."

"No?"

"No."

Teffinger wiggled his fingers in her underarms and got an explosion of laughter.

"That looks like a yes to me," he said.

Topside a half hour later, Teffinger scouted the territory to see if the caveman happened to be lurking around to see if the witness was home—the witness behind the page 5 sketch, the witness who needed to die, like Tracy White did. Teffinger didn't notice anything. He walked over to a man on a bench with a laptop thirty steps north and asked him if he'd seen anything.

He hadn't.

Teffinger headed back to the boat.

The whole bait scheme was getting more and more worrisome. The man initially made his move quickly, as Teffinger anticipated, but got away. Now he was being more cautious. He might not make a move again until he got convinced that Teffinger was no longer around.

Not good.

What if Teffinger went back to Denver and the man made his move a month from now?

R.J. JAGGER

When Teffinger got back to the boat, Fallon was topside and stepping off. "We need to find this guy," he said.

"Which guy?"

The one who killed Amanda Peterson.

And Tracy White.

And probably Michelle Berri.

And Fallon, next.

"The whole bait thing was a bad idea," he said. "This guy's going to bide his time until he's positive I'm not around and then make his move. We need a Plan B and we need it fast."

She slipped sunglasses on and they headed for the street.

On the way she flicked a lighter and said, "I lied to you before about something."

218

56

Day Six—July 17
Saturday Morning

Deja knew there was no way she could climb up twenty meters of steep rock and was about to tell Alexandra so when something flashed in her head—an image of the looter grabbing his chest.

She had killed a man.

This wasn't a game.

She looked up the face of the mountain.

"I'm going to fall and die," she said. "Promise me you won't leave my body here with the snakes."

"You'll be fine," Alexandra said.

"Promise me anyway."

"I'll drag you back to Luxor by the hair if I have to," Alexandra said. "There? Feel better?"

Deja grunted.

No, not really.

She relieved herself behind a rock cropping, took a tall drink of water, laced her shoes as tight as they would go, put on Alexandra's backpack and said, "I can't believe I'm doing this."

Then she climbed.

She was strong and coordinated but had never done anything like this before, so she went slowly and carefully, getting a feel for the rocks and the limits of her body. Ten meters up she realized that going up was the easy part. The hard part—the dangerous part—would be coming down.

She got up quicker than she thought.

She found no cave or opening.

"Now what?" she shouted down.

"Now you need to start moving the rocks out of the way and make an opening," Alexandra said. "But here's the tricky part. Don't throw the rocks down. We need to keep them up there to plug the hole back up after we leave. So just pile them to one side, if you can."

"I'm not sure there's room."

"Try."

That made things harder.

A lot harder.

She dropped her share, particularly the heavier ones, but managed to move most of them from the left to the right. Then something happened that she hoped would, but hadn't really expected.

A hole opened up.

"Got a hole," she shouted.

"Yeah, baby!"

The working got easier as more and more of her body got off the ledge and inside the opening. Then the hole got big enough for her body to get through. She didn't go through, though. Instead she took the backpack off, pulled out a flashlight, stuck her head in and looked around.

She didn't see any snakes but did see something else—death; bones and skulls, lots of them, human, right in front of her.

She pulled out as fast as she could. Then she wiped sweat off her face and shouted down to Alexandra, "Got a bunch of dead skeletons piled up just inside the entrance. Looks like six or seven of them."

"Do you see a mummy's casket?"

"Not from where I am," Deja said. "The cave angles to the right."

"Well, get in there and look. Be careful not to disturb anything."

Deja exhaled and wiped sweat out of her eyes.

She brushed the bones and skulls to the side, pushed the backpack through the hole and then followed, barely able to slither through.

Inside, the air was cool.

It should have felt nice but didn't.

It felt like death.

She stood up.

Something moved on her back.

Something alive.

Something big.

And she screamed.

57

Day Six—July 17
Saturday Afternoon

D urand headed over to the houseboat to see what was going on. It was empty, so he took a seat on a bench in the shade thirty meters north, fired up his laptop and went through the caveman's files.

A half hour later something weird happened.

Very weird.

Two people stepped off the houseboat onto the walkway; the tattoo woman and a strong looking man.

They just had sex.

It was still on their faces.

So the boat hadn't been empty after all.

The woman ducked back into the cabin, apparently forgetting something, while the man surveyed the cityscape as if looking for something. Durand pointed his face at the laptop when the man's head turned his way.

Then something unexpected happened.

The man walked over to him.

"Do you speak English?"

Durand nodded.

"Oui."

"You been here long?"

Durand shrugged and looked at his watch. "I don't know, an hour or so, I guess."

"Did you notice anyone around here paying unnecessary attention to that boat over there, as if they were staking it out or something?"

Durand shook his head.

"I've been working," he said. "Why? You had some robberies or something?"

The man turned and said over his shoulder, "No, I was just curious. Have a good one."

"You too."

As the man walked back to the boat, Durand suppressed his natural instinct, which was to close the laptop and walk away as fast as he could. Instead he forced himself to sit there and continue staring at the screen as if nothing was wrong. When the woman stepped off the boat, however, Durand pulled his hand to his face as if scratching.

The man and woman headed to the street.

As far as Durand could tell, the woman never looked his way.

He waited for ten minutes, keeping his face in the computer.

Then he closed it, stood up, stretched, and nonchalantly looked around to see if the man and woman had positioned themselves somewhere to follow him. It they had, he didn't see them. Just to be safe, however, he zigzagged through a number of streets and took a ride on the Metro before heading home.

The man must have been the one who dived at Durand the other night.

Good thing he escaped.

The guy would have crushed him.

All the risk of breaking into Anton Fornier's apartment had been for nothing, other than the opportunity to meet a cat. The man's computer files didn't shed any light on whether or not he was the one who pumped three bullets into the skull of Luc Trickett, the boxer.

Maybe he was.

Maybe he wasn't.

Same with respect to the Cairo brother, Serge.

Dead end.

Now what?

He called a man and made a request. "That's a weird one, even for you," the man said. "Let me see what I can do." Fifteen minutes later the man called back and said, "I can get you two, if you're really serious."

"I'm serious," Durand said.

"Stop over in an hour," the man said. "Bring cash."

"Always."

An hour later, Durand walked down stone stairs to a basement hideaway in an edgy neighborhood on the east fringes of the city. He knocked on a wooden door that had seen better days. A man named Jim Travenfield opened it, looking the same as always—dangerous and shifty. Durand stepped in, gave him a quick hug and asked, "You got 'em?"

The man narrowed his eyes.

Bloodshot eyes.

"Of course I got 'em," Travenfield said. "If I say I'm going to have something, I'm going to have that something. I'm not going to say I have something, and then not have that something. That's not the way I work. You know that better than anyone."

True.

"Whether I got 'em isn't the question," Travenfield said. "The question is, what the hell are you going to do with them?"

Durand shifted his feet.

"Train them to sing," he said.

"Yeah, right, you do that."

Suddenly rattling filled the air.

Durand looked that way and saw a burlap sack with a cord cinched at one end.

"That them?"

Travenfield nodded.

"That's them. Handle with care, my friend."

Durand gave the man an envelope, threw the burlap bag in the trunk of his car, pointed the front end west and flicked the radio stations, stopping on a Beatles song, "Love Me Do," which he cranked up.

A half hour later, he scouted out the houseboat from across the river and saw no signs of life. He crossed the bridge, untied the cord, strolled down the walkway and nonchalantly tossed the bag into the back of the boat.

Ten steps later, Prarie jumped into his thoughts.

He'd take her somewhere nice tonight.

He'd show her more of the Paris she'd never seen, then screw her like a rock star.

Yeah, baby.

58

Day Six—July 17
Saturday Afternoon

Fallon wanted to run down Remy Lafayette's niece—
Deja Lafayette—to confirm that the mysterious Egyptian file they found under the floater's couch actually
came from the dead archeologist's house. Teffinger, however,
talked her into sticking with the caveman case instead, on the
remote possibility that Michelle Berri was still alive, so they
ended up where the missing woman worked.

The Louvre.

Teffinger had always pictured the world-famous museum as
something that actually looked like a museum. In America, you
could usually tell when something was a museum and when it
wasn't. Not so in Paris. The Louvre ended up looking more like
an ornate palace, and not a little one, either—one that would
take two days to circle without even stopping to look at art.

Fallon must have read Teffinger's thoughts because she
said, "It's huge."

Teffinger chuckled and said, "I'm sorry, is my zipper down
again?"

She rolled her eyes and punched him on the arm.

"You wish."

They walked over to something that looked like an Egyptian pyramid, except instead of stone it was a contemporary see-through structure made entirely of black tube framing and glass.

"That's the entrance," Fallon said.

They ended up meeting with a frail, scholarly-looking, white-haired man named Guillaume, who was the head of the preservation department where Michelle Berri worked.

"Tell me about her," Teffinger said.

Guillaume collected his thoughts.

"She was a highly-gifted and dependable worker with a love of everything old. She was well liked and had no enemies," he said. "She was a nice woman. I ate lunch with her two or three times a week. If anything strange had been going on in her life, I'm not sure she would necessarily have confided in me about it, but I have a pretty high confidence level that I would have at least detected it. As far as I know, everything was normal in her life and going according to plans. Then—poof!—she was gone."

Teffinger nodded.

Right.

Poof.

Good way to put it.

"Who took her? I don't have a clue," Guillaume added. "Maybe one of her archeological friends would know."

Archeological?

Teffinger and Fallon looked at each other, shocked at the word.

"Tell me about her archeological friends," Teffinger said.

The man shook his frail white head with uncertainty. "I don't know anything about them, other than she had them and was interested in archeology."

"Did she ever take an archeology class at the university?"

"I don't know."

"Did she know an archeologist named Remy Lafayette?"

"I don't know, maybe, but she never mentioned him if she did."

They asked more questions but got no more answers.

As Teffinger and Fallon were at the door on their way out, Guillaume said, "I don't know if this means anything or not, but she was getting ready to leave her job here. Did you know that?"

Teffinger stopped and turned.

No.

He didn't know that.

"Leaving to go where?"

"Actually, to run an art gallery over in La Defense," he said. "That was a step down, in my opinion, and I told her so—but she wanted a change of scenery, something that got her more in contact with people. Our work here is detailed and solitary. In some ways, it's not that much different than creating the initial work in the first place."

Teffinger raked his hair with his fingers.

It immediately flopped back down.

"That reminds me," he said. "One of the theories I've been kicking around is that someone took Michelle as a way to get into the museum to steal art. How does that strike you?"

The man shook his head.

"Ridiculous," he said. "No offense. As far as the pieces that are being worked on down here in this department, it might be possible for someone to figure out a way to get them out of the building. But, they'd have to be at work to do it, not kidnapped and someplace else."

Outside, Teffinger told Fallon, "I'm starting to get the feeling that all these different murders are connected. Just don't ask me how."

"How?"

"I just told you, don't ask me that."

"How?"

Teffinger rolled his eyes.

"I'm being a bad girl," Fallon said. "I wouldn't blame you a bit if you made me be your sex slave again. Plus, I lied to you."

She had but the lie wasn't that big.

She'd told him before that she hadn't been with another woman before Sheila. That was a lie, actually she had. Not a lot, but she was occasionally attracted to women, if it was the right one and all the stars were in alignment. She didn't want to tell him before, because she didn't know if he'd hold it against her.

"Rest assured, the bag of goodies will be out again," Teffinger said. "In the meantime, let's run down Remy Lafayette's niece. What's her name again?"

"Deja Lafayette."

"Right, her," Teffinger said. "With any luck, she'll verify that the documents under the floater's couch came from Remy's files. With even more luck, she'll be able to tell us that Remy was one of Michelle Berri's archeological friends. Then we'll have our connection."

59

Day Six—July 17
Saturday Morning

———————

Deja smashed her back against the cave wall and rubbed violently from side to side. Three fist-sized spiders dropped to the ground. Two scampered away. The other balled up and wiggled some of its legs but not the dead ones. Deja stepped back, shivered, and then shined the flashlight ahead, to where the cave bent to the right.

She took a careful step in that direction.

Then another.

And another.

Around the corner, she found a chamber about the size of a bus. At first, nothing of interest emerged. As she shined the light and studied harder, however, several pieces of pottery took shape against the right wall, heavily encased in dirt and dust. She brushed one off and found colorful Egyptian markings.

Her heart raced.

She sensed motion behind her and pointed the flashlight that way.

She saw a spider with long hairy legs and a round brown belly, almost the same color as the rocks. At the head were stingers—poison? It didn't charge her so she let it be.

At the back of the space, the cave twisted to the left.

She walked that way and found a rough opening about the size of a door.

It led to a third space, an incredibly large space, two or three times bigger than her apartment.

She stepped inside and found pottery containers, dozens of them, much larger and more obvious than the others. Then she saw something she could hardly believe—a large object near the back wall, a rectangular object shaped like a coffin.

A sound came from it.

She stopped and concentrated but now heard nothing.

Weird.

Was she hallucinating?

Was the darkness playing a trick?

She took another step, stopped and listened again. No sounds came from anywhere. She twisted around and looked for spiders.

She saw none.

She took another step.

There it was again, the sound—

Faint, but there.

Vaguely familiar.

Then it was gone.

She stood still and swept the light. She saw nothing alive. She heard nothing. Her chest pounded. Maybe she should leave.

Then the sound came again, louder, pronounced enough that she recognized it.

The attack sound of a viper!

She shined the light at it.

A large snake was twisting violently across the cave floor directly at her.

She screamed.

The flashlight dropped to the ground, popped with a blue flash and went out.

Then the deepest, darkest blackness in the world engulfed her.

60

Day Six—July 17
Saturday Afternoon

———————

S omeone knocked on Durand's apartment door Saturday afternoon, which was weird, because that almost never happened. He looked through the peephole and saw a face he didn't expect—Nick Ringer, in the flesh, the infamous shipbuilder himself, the man with more money than some entire nations.

With him was his woman, Nodja Lefebvre, who Durand had met only once before, but even then would have crawled across a field of broken glass just to suck her toes. Her body looked just as good as he remembered, but her face more plain.

Durand let them in and said, "This is unexpected."

"Sorry to barge in like this," Ringer said, "but I need to talk to you. It's not about the investigation you're doing for me. It's about something else, a new matter." A pause. "A delicate matter."

"How delicate?"

"Very delicate," Ringer said. "I don't want to talk here. Let's take a walk."

They took a stroll through crowded streets filled with Parisians who were happily poised on the edge of an upcoming Saturday night. The first block was chitchat and then Ringer got to the point.

"I had a man doing a project for me," he said. "Unfortunately, he got killed in a traffic accident last night. I need to replace him and I need to do it fast."

"And the project is delicate—"

Ringer nodded.

"Yes."

"So what do you want from me?"

"I want you to either take over where he left off or point me to someone who can," Ringer said.

Durand cocked his head.

"What's the pay?" he asked.

Ringer told him.

"Are you serious?"

Yes.

He was.

Dead.

"I'll do it," Durand said.

"Do you want to know what it is first?"

"No, but go ahead and tell me."

Ringer told him.

Then he asked, "Do you still want to do it?"

Durand shrugged.

"Sure, sounds like fun."

After they parted, Durand went back to his apartment, fired up the laptop and logged onto the net to see who had been killed in a car accident last night.

He found one fatality, a head-on collision between two ve-
hicles north of the city.

A family of four died in one car.

In the other car, a man named Zacharie Mureau.

The father of the family had reportedly been drinking and
crossed the center line.

61

Day Six—July 17
Saturday Afternoon

———————

WHEN Deja Lafayette didn't answer her cell phone, Fallon called the law firm to see if the woman was at work, and was told by the receptionist that she was scheduled out of the office for the next week or so.

"Where?"

"I don't know."

"On holiday?"

"I don't think so."

"Why not?"

"Because everyone talks about their holidays and she didn't. This was something sudden."

Teffinger listened, not understanding, and frowned when Fallon explained it in English. He said, "Let's swing by her apartment."

Right.

On the way, they passed a red windmill that looked vaguely familiar. Teffinger read the sign—MOULIN ROUGE. "Is that the can-can place?"

It was.

"Have you ever been there?"

She had.

Everyone in Paris had, once.

"And?"

"And, it's for tourists," she said. "There are a hundred better places I can take you if you want to get your blood pumping."

Five minutes later they came to Deja's apartment.

They knocked on her door and got no answer.

"Figures," Teffinger said. "That's the way my life works." Then he tried the doorknob, found it unlocked, pushed the door open a couple of inches and shouted, "Anyone home?"

No one answered.

"Anyone here?"

Silence.

He looked at Fallon, to give her a chance to stop what he was about to do. When she didn't, he pushed the door open and stepped in.

The place was trashed.

Pictures had been taken off the wall and slit open at the back. The bed had been sliced open. Food containers had been opened and dumped in the sink—now spoiled and throwing a stench.

"This isn't good," Fallon said.

Teffinger agreed.

"This happened days ago, maybe even a week," he said. "Someone was looking for something. Something small enough to fit in a bottle of catsup."

"Or mustard."

"Right, any of your basic condiments."

They talked to two neighbors on the same floor.

Neither was aware that anything had happened or when it happened. Neither had seen Deja in a week.

Fallon called the law firm, got the same receptionist, and asked who at the firm might know where Deja Lafayette was. The receptionist didn't know.

"Who does she report to?"

"Yves Petit."

"Is he in the office today?"

"Oui, but—"

"Tell him to stay there, we're going to come down and talk to him."

"He has clients."

"We'll wait if we have to."

Yves Petit shook Teffinger's hand and then smiled at Fallon. He appeared to be in his early forties and had brown hair that he combed straight back. Teffinger immediately took him for a man who enjoyed life. Judging by the size of his office, he held a position of stature in the firm.

"You're way ahead of me here," he said to Fallon. "All I know is that this has something to do with Deja. Is she okay?"

Yes as far as they knew.

"We're trying to locate her," Fallon said. "Do you know where she is?"

Petit hesitated.

"I told her I wouldn't tell anyone," he said, "but I guess this is different. She went to Cairo."

"Cairo as in Egypt?"

Right.

That one.

"When?"

He scratched his head.

"She tied up some loose ends here at the office on Thursday morning," he said. "My understanding is that she was going to leave later that day."

"So what's in Cairo?"

He didn't know.

She wouldn't tell him.

"Something was going on," he said, "something serious. My suspicion is that she was in some kind of trouble, because she didn't want me to tell anyone where she was going."

"So maybe someone was after her?"

Yves shrugged.

"That's possible," he said. "I offered to help if she wanted it, but she didn't. And now you show up. What's going on?"

Fallon hesitated.

"We're not sure," she said.

They talked for another ten minutes. Petit gave them Deja's email address and the names and numbers of people in the office that Deja talked to on a personal level, but added, "If she would have told anyone, it would have been me."

Outside, Teffinger asked Fallon, "So what do you think?"

"I think he was being straight," she said. "He doesn't know any more than what he told us."

Teffinger shrugged and wasn't so sure.

Something about the man seemed off.

"She was going to work as late as Thursday," he said, "but her apartment got trashed a week ago, judging by the food in the sink. So where was she staying in the meantime?"

Good question, very good question.

They passed a restaurant.

Fallon grabbed Teffinger's hand and pulled him that way.

"I'm starved," she said. "Feed me."

Teffinger hesitated.

The place looked expensive, more expensive than food needed to be.

"My treat," Fallon said.

62

Day Six—July 17
Saturday

———————

Whe the flashlight went out and the world turned
black, Deja still had enough of the cave memorized to let her turn and run four or five steps.
Then she stretched her hands out and slowed, knowing she
might get bit from behind, but not wanting to hit her head and
end up on the ground.

Five seconds later she came to a wall.

Now what?

Left or right?

She went left and came to the opening.

When she got through, she saw something beautiful.

Light.

Light.

Light.

Not a lot, but enough to let her move at a good pace
through the second chamber, around the corner, to the mouth
of the cave. She pushed her backpack out the hole, got on her
stomach and slithered out.

The Egyptian sun blasted her face.

It burned her eyes.

Nothing ever felt so good.

"What'd you find?" Alexandra shouted.

"This is it," Deja said.

But there were snakes.

And she lost the flashlight.

"Okay, plug the hole and come down," Alexandra said.

They got back to Luxor without mishaps or encounters. As suspected, Alexandra's forearm was broken. She got a cast, but wouldn't let the doctor run it past her wrist or her elbow, as he wanted.

She needed to be able to climb.

They bought new flashlights.

More rope.

A digital camera.

A large knife.

And a number of burlap sacks because they had to get the snakes out of there before they could work.

"How many do you think there are?" Alexandra asked.

Deja shrugged.

"I only saw the one," she said. "But it wouldn't surprise me if there was a whole nest." She frowned and added, "The big question I have is—what do they eat when I'm not around?"

Alexandra grinned, then got serious.

"We can't get bit," she said.

"Trust me, I don't want to."

"I'm serious," Alexandra said. "Getting bit on the valley floor is one thing. But up in the cave—"

"Maybe we should think of a Plan B," Deja said. "This has gotten way bigger than just you and me."

"No it hasn't," Alexandra said. "We just need to be careful."

"I have a bad feeling."

Alexandra patted Deja's shoulder.

"I'll take the lead tomorrow, once we get inside," she said.

"Assuming you can get up."

Right.

Assuming that.

63

Day Six—July 17
Saturday Night

Saturday evening after dark, Durand picked up Prarie, drove twenty kilometers north of Paris to a place not far from where his predecessor Zacharie Mureau got killed in a head-on collision, and pulled over to the side of the road.

He powered down the window and killed the engine.

The sound of crickets permeated the air.

"I want you to know a few things about me," he said. "It's for your own good. I told you I was an investment broker. I'm not. I'm really a private investigator. I get paid well and most of what I do is legal, but not everything. Sometimes I have to find things out the hard way. Sometimes I have to do things I'd rather not. You have a right to know. That's why I'm telling you."

She asked questions.

He answered them, truthfully.

At the end she said, "None of that bothers me, and if you ever want me to help, just say the word."

Durand studied her.

"You'd have to keep it confidential."

"I already know that," she said. "Trust me, I know how to keep my mouth shut if I have to."

Durand fired up the engine.

"Let's find out," he said.

Ten minutes later he turned right on a pitch-black road and pulled over to the shoulder next to a field. "Just letting you see me stop here is secret information," he said. "Are you sure you can keep it that way?"

She kissed him.

"Yes, stop worrying."

He pulled a black bag out of the back seat, opened it and removed a black mask and a pair of latex gloves. "Wait here. I'll be back in a half hour, give or take."

"Okay."

"Don't go anywhere."

"I won't."

He kissed her, stepped out and walked briskly into the field. When he turned around fifty steps later, he couldn't see the car any longer.

The night was that black.

He got back forty minutes later, out of breath, and slid behind the wheel.

"Everything go okay?" Prarie asked.

"No problems," he said. "There's something I forgot to tell you before. I was in the house of a man named Luc Trickett, snooping around for a client the other night. While I was there, another man showed up—a hitman. I hid upstairs and he never saw me or even knew I was there. When Trickett came home, the hitman put three bullets in his head and then left. I stayed upstairs to make sure it was safe before I headed down. Unfortunately, that was a bad move. A couple of the neighbors heard the shots and came over. One was at the back door just as I was coming out. I punched him in the face, and escaped, but he saw me. He then gave the police a sketch. That sketch appeared in the paper the other day. That's why I changed my hair. Here's the important thing for you to understand. I did not kill anyone."

Silence.

"Okay."

"I need you to believe me," he said.

"I do believe you."

"Are you sure?"

"Yes."

He paused, then exhaled.

"There's one more thing," he said. "I got a look at the hitman, from behind the door upstairs. He looks a little like a caveman and I might even know who he is. But here's the twist. If he's the man I know, that means he also knows me. He might figure out that the sketch in the paper is me and might also figure out that the reason my sketch is in the paper is because someone saw me at the scene. If the pressure starts coming down on him, he'd have a lot of motivation to be sure that the one witness who could identify him wasn't alive any longer. Do you understand what I'm saying?"

"Yeah—someone might try to kill you," she said.

He nodded.

"I don't think it's going to come to that," he said. "If it is the man I know, there would need to be a lot of pressure before he'd turn on me. The more dangerous situation is if it's someone I don't know, and he finds out who I am. That guy wouldn't hesitate to put me away. But that's a long shot too, because he'd have to figure out who I was based on the sketch in the paper, which doesn't look that much like me."

"Okay."

"The reason I'm telling you this is simple," he said. "First, I want to be honest with you about everything. Second, if I do end up being a target, you could also be in danger by association. I don't want to put you in that position without you knowing about it."

"I'm not worried about it," she said.

"You sure?"

She was.

Positive.

"You'd protect me, right? If it came to it?"

Absolutely.

Without a doubt.

Without even a shadow of a doubt.

"Good enough for me," she said.

Durand smiled, fired up the engine and pointed the front end back towards the city. "I was scared I'd freak you out with all this stuff," he said.

"Sorry, it takes more than that to freak this girl out," she said. "Let's go to a bar and get drunk."

Right.

Good idea.

64

Day Six—July 17
Saturday Evening

Professor Tristan-Pierre Martin wasn't used to being in the company of someone as striking as Fallon Le Rue, and it showed in the way he diverted his eyes every time she looked at him. He taught archeology at the university, together with Remy Lafayette. He was slight of build, slight of looks, and hid his face behind round John Lennon glasses and an overgrown moustache that any normal person would have whacked off years ago. His office was cluttered with books and papers and dusty corners. Teffinger looked at it with a frown and would have paid half his salary on the spot to make the window bigger.

"I get Remy's leftovers," the professor said. "Everyone signs up for him and then gets spilled into my class when his fills up."

Fallon smiled.

"I doubt that," she said. "Thanks for seeing us on such short notice, especially on a Saturday night. We really appreciate it."

The professor chuckled.

"Yeah, I had to put my harem on hold, but it's not like they won't be there when I get back."

Fallon smiled.

"Let's see what you have," he said.

Fallon looked for a clean spot on the desk to set the papers, found none, and handed them to him. They were the papers and photographs from the mysterious file found under the floater's couch earlier today. Now, however, each piece was individually sealed and marked in a clear evidence bag.

As they suspected, the notes were written in Egyptian.

The professor read them out loud, fluently.

They turned out to be field notes dated eighteen years ago. Although the author wasn't identified, he referred to his ten-year-old daughter Alexandra.

Fallon turned to Teffinger. "If they're actually eighteen years old, that would put this Alexandra at twenty-eight now."

Teffinger agreed.

The notes talked about an archeological investigation that the author, his wife and their daughter Alexandra, had been doing in an area west of the Valley of the Kings, in Egypt. Although the notes described the area with some particularity, there was no reference to them finding anything. About the only thing of real interest was on the last page, which talked about the father getting bit by a viper at the base of a craggy mountain cliff.

"If there's something here that I'm supposed to be seeing, I'm not seeing it," Teffinger said.

"Me either," Fallon said.

"Do you see something we don't?" Teffinger asked the professor.

No.

He didn't.

The notes were nothing more than a daily diary of random wanderings by someone that went nowhere, eighteen years ago.

"We're assuming that these notes were in Remy Lafayette's possession at the time he got killed," Teffinger said. "Why would he have them?"

The professor shrugged.

"No reason that I can see," he said. "He can write Egyptian but that's not his handwriting. Whoever wrote this, it was someone other than him."

The ten or twelve photographs were easy to explain. They were photographs of the inventory lists from the tomb that was discovered in the Valley of the Kings six months ago.

"That's what Remy was working on before he died," the professor said, "finding the missing treasure."

Missing treasure?

What missing treasure?

"You don't know?"

No.

He didn't.

So the professor told him.

A tomb was discovered six months ago, a tomb remarkably well preserved, a tomb totally intact except for one small thing, namely all of the treasure was missing. "It's never shown up anywhere in the world," the professor said.

On the drive back to the houseboat, Teffinger said, "At the risk of seeming like the most boring person in the world, especially on a Saturday night, what I'd really like to do tonight if you don't mind is just chill out on the boat and get to bed early."

That was fine with Fallon.

"I don't need to be entertained, if that's what you're worried about."

When they got to the boat, Teffinger spotted something out of place—a burlap sack on the deck in the middle of the sitting area, empty. Fallon took it, threw it away and said, "Some people think that this is just a giant floating garbage can."

They brought a flat-panel TV outside, popped in a DVD—King Kong—and cuddled up in the cushions.

Teffinger had half his brain on the movie and half on what the professor told them.

"My neighbor has a smart dog," he said.

Fallon looked at him.

"Where did that come from?"

Teffinger chuckled.

"What he does is put the dog on a rope and then loops that rope around a tree," Teffinger said. "Then he puts a bowl of food in front of the dog, just out of reach. No matter how strong the dog pulls, he can't get to the food. Now, most dogs in that situation would starve to death, but not this dog. He eventually figures out that to get to the food, he actually has to go in the opposite direction first and un-loop himself around the tree."

Fallon wrinkled her forehead.

"And you're telling me this, because?"

"Because we need to be as smart as that dog," he said. "I'm starting to think that the best way for us to get to the bottom of everything here in Paris is to go to Cairo."

"So Cairo is the tree, in your example."

Teffinger clinked his beer can against her glass of wine.

"Bingo," he said.

"And you and me are the dogs," she said.

"Well, yeah."

"You're such a poet, Teffinger," she said. "Has anyone ever told you that?"

He nodded.

"It's a curse I have. Same as T.S. Elliot."

He looked down at his foot but it was too dark to see anything

"What's the matter?" Fallon asked.

"Nothing, I just thought I felt something for a second."

65

Day Seven—July 18
Sunday Morning

Deja and Alexandra made it to the cave just before daybreak. No one had been there since they left, as far as they could tell. Deja climbed up first, opened the hole and pulled up all their stuff with a rope. Then Alexandra tied the rope around her chest and climbed as best she could with a broken arm while Deja pulled.

She made it.

So cool.

They curled the rope up.

Directly inside the mouth were lots of spiders. "Don't worry about them," Alexandra said. "They're not poisonous or anything. They're probably the reason the vipers are coming in."

To eat them?

Right.

That.

"Okay, snake time," Alexandra said.

They swept the front area thoroughly with their flashlights

and found no snakes.

The cave bent to the right and opened into a second chamber about the size of a bus. "There's some of the pottery I told you about," Deja said, bouncing her light on it.

"Cool."

They saw no snakes.

"The big room's through that door," Deja said. "That's where the viper was."

They entered cautiously and panned the room with their lights, including the walls and ceiling, but saw no snakes.

"They're probably behind the pots," Alexandra said.

Deja swallowed.

"Maybe there was just that one and he left," she said.

Silence.

"Don't stick your hands anywhere you can't see."

"Don't worry."

"That includes our stuff," Alexandra said. "Don't reach into your backpack unless you look first."

Right.

Good idea.

Suddenly they saw something move near the far end of the room.

"Company."

Alexandra got one of the burlap bags out of her backpack, set it on the ground, then turned off the flashlight and set it next to the bag. "Okay, we're going to walk towards it. Keep the light right in its eyes."

"That's not the one I saw yesterday," Deja said. "It's smaller."

They walked across the room.

Slowly.

The snake was about three meters in front of the coffin. Deja veered to the right, holding the light high and keeping it in the reptile's eyes, while Alexandra stepped to the left.

The snake curled up and raised its head.

Fair warning.

Fixated on the light.

Making that terrible sound.

FFFFFFFF—

Alexandra slowly worked her way behind it.

Now within striking distance if it turned.

The reptile bobbed its head back and forth. Alexandra gauged the rhythm and then reached for the back of its neck with every ounce of speed she had.

She got it and pulled it up until it dangled.

It twisted violently.

"Get the bag!"

Deja did.

Alexandra dropped it inside and immediately pulled the drawstring and tied it.

"I can't believe you did that," Deja said.

"Me either, you should feel my heart."

Suddenly something moved on the floor, another snake, a bigger one, not more than two steps away, coming right at them.

Deja screamed and Alexandra swung the bag at it.

66

Sunday

————————

Durand slept until noon on Sunday, still dull from too much alcohol last night, but not to the point of pain or dysfunction. He showered with Prarie and ended up getting a nice blowjob under the spray. Then he took her out for coffee and croissants and felt the need for culture.

They went to the Musee d'Orsay and got lost in the magic of the masters.

Renoir.

Monet.

Degas.

Sisley.

Cassatt.

Van Gogh.

"I've always wanted to do something like this that would live on after I died," he said.

"Why?"

He shrugged.

"I don't know—just to leave my mark, I guess. Prove I was

here."

She locked her arm through his.

"You can leave your mark on me," she said.

He smiled.

"That'll work too."

Yeah?

Yeah.

Five minutes later, he was admiring Paul Gauguin's "Breton Peasant Women" when Nicholas Ringer called and asked, "Everything go okay last night?"

"Yeah, no problems."

"Good. I wired some money to your account."

"I trust you."

"Yeah, I know, but you trust money more."

Durand chuckled.

"Maybe a little."

When he hung up, Prarie asked, "Who was that?"

"Work."

"Just so long as it isn't another woman," she said.

"Why?"

She hugged him.

"Because I want you all to myself."

"Well you have me all to yourself, so there."

"Good."

"Yeah?"

"Yeah."

67

Day Seven—July 18
Sunday Morning

Teffinger got up before daybreak Sunday morning and slipped out of bed, careful to not wake Fallon, who looked more dead than sleeping. He popped in his contacts and headed outside for a jog.

The air was nice, cool without being chilly.

Traffic didn't exist.

The maniac drivers were still asleep.

The river was peaceful and reflected the city lights with an artist's touch. Teffinger ran across the bridge and opened up the pace, letting his legs stretch and his lungs burn.

Archeology.

Archeology.

Archeology.

Everywhere he turned, there it was.

A tomb was discovered in the Valley of the Kings six months ago. The treasure from that tomb was missing. Archeologist Remy Lafayette was trying to figure out where it was and ended up murdered. His files on the project were missing.

Some of those files ended up under the couch of a lowlife scumbag named Pascal Lambert, who got shot in the chest, and got his head and hands cut off and thrown into the woods, by at least two people, and ended up floating in the river, seriously dead.

Remy Lafayette's niece, Deja, had her apartment torn apart and then she mysteriously disappeared to Cairo, not wanting anyone to know where she was. Some of the files found under the lowlife's couch dealt with archeological explorations undertaken eighteen years ago.

Amanda Peterson got her eyes gouged out in Denver.

Tracy White—the witness—got her eyes gouged out in Paris, obviously by the same man.

Tracy's roommate, Michelle Berri, was taken by that same man.

Michelle Berri was into archeology.

Teffinger's heart raced.

Now that he had it all organized, there was only one conclusion—the man who killed Amanda Peterson and Tracy White, and who took Michelle Berri, was somehow connected to these archeological events. In fact, now that Teffinger thought about it, maybe the man's initial interest had been in Michelle Berri the whole time and not in Tracy White at all. Maybe he just happened to stumble across her by incredibly good luck.

Everything was clear.

Teffinger needed to get to the missing treasure because that's where the killer was headed.

Back at the houseboat, he shook Fallon until she woke up. "Come on, sleepyhead. We need to go to Cairo."

Then he headed to the shower.

She joined him three minutes later and said, "Lather me up," while she washed her hair.

He did; and told her his theory.

She wasn't impressed.

"The connection's thin," she said. "True, there's a lot of archeological stuff going on, but the only link between that and your eye-gouger is a rumor that Michelle Berri was into archeology. We haven't even verified that's true yet."

"You don't believe the guy down at the Louvre?"

"Of course I do, but we haven't established any details yet."

"We don't have time," he said. "Everything's going down in Cairo. I can feel it."

She shook her head, still not impressed.

"I'll go," she said, "but only because someone needs to keep you out of trouble."

Teffinger smiled and slapped her ass.

68

Day Seven—July 18
Sunday Morning

———————

The viper stopped when the bag hit it. Then it curled up, bobbed its head, hissed, and disappeared behind the coffin. A quick sweep of the cave with flashlights didn't show any more charging reptiles.

"That one scares me," Alexandra said. "Let's just let him be for right now."

That was fine with Deja, more than fine.

Alexandra surveyed the cave. There were several dozen large pottery containers, a lot more than she expected. She dusted one off and found perfectly preserved markings.

"The pottery alone is worth a fortune," she said.

She lifted the top, keeping a distance just in case there were snakes inside.

There weren't.

"Look at this," she said.

Deja swept the ground with light and then walked over.

The entire jar was filled with gold inscribed coins.

Alexandra reached in, pulled a handful out and handed

them to Deja. "Those are gold," she said. "Stick them in your pocket—wait, count them first."

Five.

There were five.

Shiny.

Brand new.

Perfectly scribed with detailed markings.

Alexandra took five for herself and said, "That's enough to retire on in comfort, right there."

"There must be hundreds of them, just in this pot alone," Deja said.

True.

"Three thousand, according to the inventory list. Before we do anything else, I want to take pictures of this place and get the scene documented," Alexandra said.

She got her camera out of the backpack—a digital with a flash, not nearly as good as the situation deserved, but all she had— and took pictures, dozens of them, from all angles.

Deja watched for snakes.

"I had no idea how massive and heavy all this stuff was," Alexandra said. "In hindsight, the father wouldn't have been able to get it all here on his own, not without making a whole lot of trips. My guess is that the skeletons by the entrance are the men who were used to break into the pharaoh's tomb in the first place. Then the guy used them to get all the stuff here. Then he killed them."

"How?"

"I don't know."

"It would be one against six or seven," Deja said.

"We'll look at the bones later, maybe they'll tell us something," Alexandra said. "This guy was smart, I got to hand him that. Maybe he made a side deal with two of the guys, to give them the shares of whoever else they killed. Then the guy got behind them and stuck a knife in each one of their backs at the same time."

Deja pictured it and shivered.

"All that killing so his son can have a nice afterlife," she said. "Twisted thinking, don't you think?"

Yes.

Very.

The coffin was a plain wooden box, but very large. Alexandra shined her light at the ground around it, saw no snakes and walked over. "If my hunch is right, this is just a shell. The real coffin's inside. That's where the golden mask is. Are you ready to find out?"

"Yes."

Alexandra hesitated.

"What? What's wrong?"

"I just wish my dad had come up here," she said. "He searched for something like this his whole life. He was so close. This is his find, not ours."

"Agreed," Deja said. "We'll give him all the credit."

Alexandra hugged her.

"Are you serious? Because if you are, that means a lot—"

"I'm dead serious," Deja said.

The lid was sealed tighter than Alexandra expected. That was bad for getting it off, but good in that snakes and spiders probably hadn't gotten in.

She pried it open with a knife, taking her time, being careful to not break it.

Inside was a perfectly preserved mummy casket.

Colorful.

Ornate.

Looking brand new.

With a solid-gold head.

"Cool." Deja said.

"Cool?"

"Right."

"This one is way bigger than Tut's," Alexandra said. "More intricate, too. You're looking at the most significant archeological find in the last three thousand years and your reaction is, cool?"

Deja grinned.

"Right, cool," she said. "That's what I said and I'm sticking to it."

Alexandra punched her in the arm.

"Okay, cool it is then," she said. "That's the first word spoken after this was found and that's the word that will go down in the history books."

Cool.

Alexandra wiggled her light on the burlap bag. "Do me a favor, will you? Take that bad boy and set him out in the front of the cave. We'll lower him down when we leave and set him loose somewhere on our way back. Right now, I'm afraid we're going to get distracted and step on him."

"You want me to touch that thing?"

Alexandra picked up the bag and handed it to Deja.

"Here, have fun."

Deja took it and headed towards the other end of the chamber.

"You owe me one," she said.

"Put it on my tab."

Deja carried the bag at the end of a straight arm, as far away from her body as she could. She worked her way to the front entrance of the cave and then bent down to scoot the bag through the hole.

Suddenly a face appeared in front of her.

The face of a man.

A dark face.

A mean face.

Just outside the hole.

He said something rough and loud and animated and pointed a gun at her eyes.

69

Day Seven—July 18
Sunday Afternoon

WHile Prarie made a stop in the museum restroom, something weird happened to Durand as he waited—he saw the caveman taxi driver, Anton Fornier, walking towards the exit, arm-in-arm with a very nice woman--a woman out of Fornier's league, a woman who was non-caveman-like in every way, a sexy woman.

Durand ran over to say hello.

Then something even weirder happened.

The caveman wasn't Fornier at all, he was a different caveman. Durand stopped short and realized something. The man had a striking resemblance to the hitman who planted three bullets in the boxer's head. In fact, he had as much resemblance to the man as Fornier did.

When they pushed through the exit, Durand followed.

He didn't like leaving Prarie alone, but had no choice.

The caveman and woman stopped at a sidewalk café and talked for an hour over coffee. It didn't appear that the waiter knew who they were. The man paid cash.

From there, they took a walk down the Seine, a long walk.

Durand dropped behind as far as he could.

He had been on their tail too long.

Sooner or later one of them was bound to turn to the other and say, "Didn't we see that guy somewhere an hour ago?"

"Yeah, I think you're right."

It took another hour but they finally did something beautiful.

They walked to a parking lot, got in a car and took off.

The woman drove.

Durand jotted down her license plate number.

Got you.

70

Day Seven—July 18
Sunday

———————

On the flight to Cairo, Teffinger tried to not grip the armrests too tight or let his forehead sweat too much. It must not have done any good because Fallon patted his arm and said, "Lots of people are afraid to fly. Don't worry about it—you're still a stud."

He exhaled.

"Thanks."

She smiled and added, "Ninety percent, anyway. Did you have a bad experience or something?"

Teffinger shrugged.

"Not really," he said. "I guess it's just a combination of not trusting machines and not trusting people, especially when there's gravity involved. When I'm in something that's moving, I need to be behind the wheel. I know what I'm looking at and what I'm thinking and all that. When someone else is driving, I have no idea what's going through their mind."

"You're okay when I drive," Fallon said.

Silence.

"Right?"

"Sure."

"You liar, you're not."

"No, I am—90 percent."

She punched him on the arm.

"So what did your chief say when you told him you wanted to go to Egypt?"

Teffinger grunted.

"The chief and I have an understanding," he said. "I do stuff without telling him and then beg for forgiveness later."

"So he doesn't even know?"

Teffinger shook his head.

"He sleeps better that way."

When they got to Cairo, they realized they still weren't in the right place. They really needed to be at the Valley of the Kings, because that was the area described in the notes—the 18-year-old notes, the ones Remy Lafayette had, the ones that meant something to him for some reason.

Although they weren't at their final destination yet, no harm done. There hadn't been a direct flight from Paris to Luxor in any event.

They hopped on a two-prop shuttle.

The pilot jumpstarted the engines and pointed the nose south towards Luxor.

The aircraft bucked and rattled and twisted. "This thing's falling apart," Teffinger said. "I have a 20-year-old refrigerator that can fly better."

"Relax."

"I mean it. The wings are going to fall off."

"Relax," Fallon said, "before your stud factor goes down to

80 percent."

Teffinger grunted.

"Where does it need to be, for bedroom privileges?"

"Eighty-five percent, minimum."

"I better shut up then," he said.

"Exactly."

Below, the Nile cut a green swath of oasis through a dangerous, barren land. Teffinger thought he saw a crocodile sunning itself on a muddy bank, but wasn't sure.

The right engine sputtered.

"Did you hear that?"

"Hear what?"

"The engine."

No.

She didn't.

"Eighty percent and dropping."

Teffinger looked around. The aircraft had twenty or so seats and half were filled. No one else seemed nervous. They all seemed like they'd done this a hundred times and everything was normal.

Okay.

Calm down.

The engine sputtered again.

Teffinger tried to ignore it.

He must have had a look on his face because Fallon said, "Seventy-five percent."

Then the engine conked out completely.

Teffinger put the armrests into a death grip and waited for the engine to catch. The pilot was doing something animated with the controls and muttering under his breath.

The plane started to lose altitude.

Then the engine caught.

The pilot exhaled loudly.

And the nose rose.

"I'll swim the river back to Cairo before I get on this death-trap again," Teffinger said.

"I'm starting to see your point." She looked at her watch. "We land in forty-five minutes."

The engine sputtered again.

And conked out.

The plane dropped.

Come on you piece of crap.

Start.

But the engine didn't start.

And the plane dropped farther.

And farther.

And farther.

The Nile was in good focus now. Teffinger could make out the swirls in the water and the details of the banks. Three people in a boat stared up. At this rate they'd crash in another minute.

The pilot turned.

Frantic.

And said something animated.

Teffinger didn't understand the language but knew what he was saying.

They were going down.

Hold on.

He pulled his seatbelt as tight as it would go and told Fallon, "Get ready!"

She gripped his hand.

Hard.

Ten meters off the ground, the engine caught and the plane

rose. The pilot shouted something ecstatic and waved his arms. Everyone in the plane cheered.

Then the engine cut off again.
   The plane dropped.
   It skipped on the surface of the Nile.
   Then the river grabbed it.

71

Day Seven—July 18
Sunday Morning

———————

The man would shoot her in the face if she moved, Deja knew that, so she stayed still. The man waved the gun at the burlap, meaning for her to set the bag down.

She obeyed.

The man grabbed it and pulled it out the hole.

Then he bounced it up and down to feel the weight.

He looked at Deja, smiled, and said something.

This was his now.

He untied the top and reached in.

Then he screamed and pulled his hand out. The viper came with it, its fangs still planted in the man's flesh. He recoiled backwards. Someone behind him shouted something. Then the man's face dropped out of sight and the sound of two people screaming disappeared down the mountainside.

Deja scrambled backwards, not sure where the snake was.

Suddenly Alexandra appeared behind her.

"What's going on?"

Deja told her.

Then Alexandra got down on her stomach, looked for the snake, didn't see it, and slowly eased her way out the hole. She looked below and then told Deja, "Get your hat and two bottles of water. Leave everything else there."

Deja did as she was told.

Then they climbed down.

Two men were on the ground, broken and dead.

The burlap bag was next to them.

Empty.

A gun was next to it.

Two camels were tied to a rock twenty steps away, watching with curious eyes. Alexandra went through the men's pockets, front and back, and said, "No cell phones. I don't think they called anyone."

"Who are they?"

"My guess? Locals, scouting around on the off chance that someone is out here finding treasure," Alexandra said. "Either that or they were going to rape us. We need to get them out of here."

Deja didn't understand.

"We found the treasure," she said. "Why don't you just call your contacts at the government and let them handle everything at this point?"

Alexandra frowned.

"It's not that simple."

"Why not?"

"We have two dead bodies, for one thing."

"So what? That's their problem. We didn't do anything wrong."

"It doesn't matter," Alexandra said. "They're a complication and this needs to be complication-free."

"I don't get it."

"Just trust me. I know what I'm doing."

At Alexandra's insistence, they draped the bodies over the backs of the camels, got in the saddles and rode ten kilometers west, where they stopped at the base of a cliff not too different from the one where the cave was.

They positioned the bodies at the base of the cliff, stripped the camels and let them loose.

"They'll find their way back to the Nile."

Then they walked back towards the cave.

The water disappeared halfway back.

They got headaches and felt nauseous.

They made it back, but barely—and the sun wasn't letting up, not a bit.

"I don't have enough strength to climb up," Deja said.

Alexandra didn't either, not even close.

They crawled into the shade, laid down in the dirt and closed their eyes.

72

Day Seven—July 18
Sunday Afternoon

After Durand got a license plate number, he couldn't find Prarie. She wasn't at the end of a cell phone, because she was the only person in the world who didn't have one, nor was she at the museum, her apartment, his apartment or the café.

Damn it.

Where was she?

Maybe she was in her apartment, but was too pissed to open the door.

He went back and knocked again.

No one answered.

"Prarie, I had an emergency, I'm sorry," he said.

No answer came.

"Come on, open up, let me explain."

No answer.

He went home and ran down the license plate number. The vehicle belonged to someone named Chantal Thomas, who had an address in a nice residential neighborhood south of the city. Durand grabbed a pair of binoculars, hopped in his car and swung by to see if there was another vehicle in the driveway, meaning the caveman's. There wasn't. In fact, Chantal's car wasn't there either.

Her house was nice.

The woman had money.

When Durand got back to his building, Prarie was sitting on the front steps. He sat down next to her, hugged her and said, "I had an emergency. I had to take off right away. I'm really sorry."

She hugged him back.

"I figured something like that happened," she said.

He explained in detail—he saw a caveman who might have been the guy who killed Luc Trickett. He had no choice but to follow.

She wasn't mad and hadn't been avoiding him, either. She'd used the opportunity to run a few errands and buy groceries.

Suddenly a cop car pulled up.

Two cops got out.

Durand instinctively covered his face.

The cops walked past him, into the building, and up the stairs.

Durand grabbed Prarie and walked away from the building. "Someone must have seen that sketch in the paper and called in with my name," he said.

Prarie squeezed his hand.

"You can stay at my place tonight."

73

When the Nile grabbed the plane, Teffinger's head shot forward and slammed into something. Within seconds, however, almost all movement stopped. He felt blood in his mouth but he wasn't dead.

Fallon wasn't either.

People were screaming.

The pilot was slumped over, not moving.

Water was pouring through the windshield.

"Can you swim?"

Fallon looked hysterical.

"No!"

"When we get in the water, I'm going to turn you away from me and grab you around the chest," he said. "Your head will go under but it will come back up. Do you understand?"

"Nick! Don't let me die!"

"I won't."

He grabbed her hand and pulled her to the front of the plane. Water was coming in, but slowly, not with the force of a waterfall, not so fast that they couldn't go against it. He kicked the rest of the glass out, muscled through, and pulled Fallon out onto the nose. He pulled off his shoes. The bank was forty meters away.

"Turn around!"

She did.

He wrapped his right arm around her chest and jumped into the water.

They went under.

Way under.

The water was cold and powerful.

Their heads punched up through the surface. He got as horizontal as he could and kicked with his legs towards the bank. His free arm couldn't do much except keep them from sinking.

They got to the shore.

Alive.

"Stay here!" he shouted.

Then he pulled off his pants and shirt, ran down the bank to where the plane had drifted, dove into the water and swam overhand towards it.

He couldn't breathe when he got there.

He went through the windshield anyway.

Everyone was still inside, screaming.

The cabin was half filled with water, up to the armrests, and the plane was on the verge of going under.

A girl about eight was crying hysterically.

Teffinger unbuckled her seatbelt, swept her up with one arm and carried her to the front. He waved his hand.

"Come on! Get out! Everyone! Now!"

Then he muscled through the windshield, jumped into the water and swam for everything he was worth.

He got to shore.

The girl was coughing up water but didn't need mouth-to-mouth.

"Stay here!" he said.

Then he ran down the bank and dived back in.

74

Day Seven—July 18
Sunday Afternoon

Deja woke up groggy, hot and sore, but most of all with a sandpaper tongue that felt like it had been lying out in the sun the whole time. She realized she had fallen asleep on the valley floor and looked for snakes. She saw none and shook Alexandra. "I need water or I'm going to die."

Alexandra muscled to her feet and surveyed the horizon.

Then she said, "We need to get that hole plugged before someone ends up out here searching for those two guys."

They climbed up.

And each drank a full water bottle, which left them with one apiece, enough to get back to town alive. A lot of the stuff they could leave in the cave—the flashlights, shovel, rope, food and burlap bags. They put the water bottles, the camera and some of the food into their backpacks. Alexandra went down, using the rope for support. Deja pulled the rope up, stuck it in the cave, plugged the hole with rocks and climbed down.

Then they walked east towards Luxor with the sun at their

backs.

On the way, Deja said, "I still don't understand what we're doing. We found the treasure. How come you're not calling your
contacts at the government so they can come and get it before
someone else does?"

Alexandra exhaled.

"I told you, it's not that easy."

Deja stopped walking.

"It seems that easy to me," she said. "The only reason I
came here in the first place was to get the treasure into safe
hands so the looters would give up and leave me alone. Every
minute you waste is another minute I'm at risk; and you too,
for that matter."

Alexandra got a distant look.

"That's not the only reason you came," she said.

"No?"

"No. You also came to find out who killed Remy," Alexandra said, "or at least I think you did. If we turn the treasure
over to the government, the looters will evaporate. They'll just
go on living their little lives as if nothing happened. Do you
really want them sitting in a bar drinking beer and telling jokes,
while Remy rots away in a coffin?"

They walked in silence.

"Maybe that's something you can live with," Alexandra added. "If it is, then I'm a different person than you. That guy
you shot, in my apartment, he would have killed me. There's
no question in my mind. True, he's dead, but his little friends
aren't, and they're just as guilty as if they had been there themselves with their fingers on my throat."

"So this is about revenge?" Deja asked.

"It's about two things," Alexandra said. "Getting the treasure to the government is the first one. Revenge is the second. If we turn the treasure over now, we only get it half done. If we play our cards right, though, we can do both."

Alexandra stopped walking, put her hands on Deja's shoulders and looked her in the eyes.

"Don't you want to bring Remy's killers to justice?"

Deja thought about it and realized something.

Yes.

She did.

She nodded to prove it.

"Yes."

"Good."

"So how do we do it?" she asked.

"I don't know yet," Alexandra said. "That's what I'm trying to figure out."

They walked.

The sun beat down.

The heat made their legs heavy.

They drank the water, down to a mouthful, but didn't drink it all because of the pressure of knowing there was none left.

"We need to draw them in," Alexandra said.

"You mean the looters?"

"Right. The best way to do that is with the treasure," Alexandra said. "We need to be absolutely sure they don't get it though. That's the tricky part."

Agreed.

"We also need to be sure they don't capture us, or even one of us for that matter."

Agreed again.

"Maybe you should back out at this point and let me handle it," Alexandra said.

Deja watched their shadows walking.

"How many times would you be dead right now if I wasn't around?"

Alexandra grunted.

"Point taken," she said. "But likewise, remember."

"I remember."

75

S unday night after dark, Durand and Prarie swung by Chantal Thomas' house and found one vehicle in the driveway—hers. They parked a couple of hundred meters away, doubled back on foot and looked in the windows to see if the caveman was inside. They saw no one but the windows were open and they heard noises upstairs, strange noises.

"What's going on?" Prarie asked.

Durand didn't know.

"Come on."

They worked their way through the shadows, along the edge of the house, to the back. There they found a double deck, with one level coming off the first floor and another above. Stairs led to the upper level.

They walked up on cat feet.

A sliding glass door was partially opened.

A faint light came from inside.

They peeked in.

The caveman was in a chair, fully clothed.

The woman was naked and draped across his lap, with her ass in the air, being spanked. After each slap she said, "Thank you master. Give me another please."

Sometimes he would spank her right away.

Other times he would run his hand over her flesh.

Caressingly.

Lovingly.

Letting her anticipate it.

Building the moment.

Then, slap!

They watched for five minutes and then headed back to the car. On the way Prarie said, "You can't believe how horny I am right now."

Durand didn't know if the man lived there, but had the feeling he didn't, meaning the woman might eventually drive him home. So they waited in the car down the street for an hour.

Then they gave up.

He took Prarie back to her apartment and, at her insistence, draped her naked body over his lap and spanked her. Then they made love like rock stars.

Prarie hit the sack.

Durand tucked her in, then headed out to do some night work.

He went down to the houseboat and walked once down the opposite side of the river. The boat was dark and had no signs of life. Was the woman sprawled out somewhere inside with fang marks in her face and a head twice its normal size?

There was no telling.

Durand headed back to Prarie's and crawled into bed.

She cuddled up.

76

Day Seven—July 18
Sunday

Teffinger got two more people out of the plane before it disappeared under the surface of the Nile—a small boy, about three, who turned out to be the brother of the girl; and a woman, about thirty, who turned out to be the mother of the two kids. Everyone else died, as far as he knew.

Boats showed up.

Helicopters appeared.

Ambulances and police cars screeched to a stop on a road to the west.

People were everywhere.

He didn't want to be there. He wanted to be somewhere quiet where he could process what happened and figure out if he should have done something differently, or better, or smarter. He needed to get an idea whether or not he could have pulled another person out. Until he knew the answer to that, he'd have no peace.

"Nick, are you okay?" Fallon asked.

He shrugged.

"I'm fine."

"You don't look fine."

Someone showed up who spoke fairly good English and ended up being the interpreter. Lots of different people had lots of different questions.

Teffinger answered as best he could, patiently, because he understood how investigations worked.

By the time it was all said and done, everyone was treating him like a god. But he didn't feel like a god. He felt like a mortal who was still alive while other people weren't.

The police gave him and Fallon a ride to Luxor. Fallon had nothing left except the clothes on her back. Her purse, passport, driver's license, money and everything else were gone. Teffinger, luckily, had his wallet, but that was it.

He stared out the window and saw lots of sugarcane fields and locals with hard lives.

On the way, Fallon said, "I kept waiting for the mother to come over and thank you. I'm totally shocked she didn't."

"She thanked me," Teffinger said.

"She did? I never saw it—"

"She looked at me, it was in her eyes."

"But still, you'd think—"

"She didn't need to," Teffinger said. "She understood and I understood. She needed to concentrate on her husband."

In Luxor, they checked into a hotel and bought clothes and necessities. Then, with three bottles of wine and glasses of ice in hand, they wandered outside until they found a quiet shady spot. Even though it was early evening, the air still blistered. That was fine, though, because it sweated the crash out of Teffinger's body. They didn't talk much. Then the wine loosened Teffinger's brain and he let words out as the sun got lower and the shadows grew longer.

Fallon listened with her arm around his shoulders.

By the time the second bottle was gone, Teffinger knew he had done everything he could. There was nothing he could have done differently to save another person. In hindsight, he'd been more than lucky to get the mother out.

He exhaled.

He still felt bad but didn't deserve any guilt.

77

Day Eight—July 19
Monday Morning

Deja got shaken awake Monday morning before sunrise. It turned out that Alexandra had come up with a grand plan during the night. The first part of that plan called for them to go to Cairo. So that's what they did, taking a two-prop plane. Besides one man in the back, they were the only passengers. The pilot looked nervous.

Weird.

Where was everyone?

Besides the normal rattling and shaking, and the occasional sputtering of one of the engines, the trip was uneventful. The pilot looked relieved when they landed and said something to Alexandra in Egyptian.

"What'd he say?" Deja asked.

"He said, See, no crash."

A man named Amaury picked them up at the airport.

He was about thirty, bigger than most, with strong arms, piercing blue eyes, a white smile and a rough, dangerous bad-boy look. He wore beige pants, black shoes and a blue cotton shirt. He gave Deja a sideways glance, then put his arms around Alexandra, spun her around and kissed her on the mouth like he owned her.

"You taste like I remember," he said in French.

"Then you have a good memory, because it's been three years."

Suddenly he turned and looked directly into Deja's eyes. She felt like prey being studied by a predator. "How does your friend taste?" he asked Alexandra.

"I don't know, try her."

The man pulled Deja's stomach to his, locked her in place with those muscular arms, and kissed her—on the mouth, like a lover.

He didn't pull away until she stopped struggling. Then he laughed, released her and told Alexandra, "She's nice, this friend of yours." To Deja, "What's your name?"

She pushed him on the chest.

"None of your business."

He smiled.

"*None of your business*," he said. "You have nice eyes, *None of your business*. But we need to work on your kissing."

They got in his car with Alexandra in the front and Deja in the back, and headed east into increasingly thicker Cairo traffic.

Alexandra fed him information on the way, telling him about Remy Lafayette's search for the lost treasure, his murder, the attack on Alexandra by a man named Pascal Lambert—one of the looters, who ended up shot.

Amaury turned and smiled at Deja.

"I'm impressed," he said.

"No one knows," Deja said. "I didn't know Alexandra was going to tell you."

He looked sympathetic.

"Your secret is safe with me, don't worry. I've been forced to do the same thing myself on occasion. Do you want names?"

No.

She didn't.

"Fada Sayyid, Istanbul, Turkey, last year," he said. "Now you have my secret too; one of them, anyway. But know this. I never killed anyone who didn't have it coming." He winked. "Same as you."

At street level in an edgy section of Cairo, Amaury stuck a key in the lock of an inconspicuous wooden door next to a laundry. They stepped inside. The man slid two deadbolts into place and led them down a cinderblock stairwell. At the bottom he unlocked a thick steel door that led to a large, underground space. Along the back wall were freestanding metal shelves. A number of cardboard boxes sat on those shelves.

Different shapes.

Different sizes.

He sat down at a scratched wooden desk.

Alexandra and Deja took chairs in front.

The man looked at Alexandra and said, "Okay, let's see what you got."

Alexandra reached into her purse.

She pulled out one of the gold coins from the cave and carefully set it in front of him.

"I'll be damned," he said.

Amaury made his living in the black market, buying and selling ancient artifacts.

It was a dangerous profession but lucrative, and his blood never fell asleep.

Alexandra's proposition was simple. Amaury would put the coin on the market and pretend it was for sale. Because it was specifically listed on the tomb's inventory list, and because it was genuine on its face, there would be no doubt that it came from the lost treasure. If the looters had half an ear on the market—which they must—they would be lured in.

The coin was the bait.

Amaury cast a serious eye on Alexandra. "This won't just draw the people you're looking for. Every lowlife on the face of the earth will raise an eyebrow."

Alexandra shrugged.

She didn't care.

"Just be sure you get the right people," she said. "You know that Pascal Lambert was one of them. You need to figure out a way to use that information to be sure you have the right people."

He nodded.

"I already have a plan," he said. "And now we get to the good part. What exactly do you want me to do to them, once I find them?"

Alexandra looked at Deja and said, "They killed Remy."

The implication was obvious—an eye for an eye.

Part of Deja thought that was fair.

Another part didn't.

"I know," she said, "but—"

Silence.

Alexandra said to Amaury, "Once you know who they are, call me. We'll regroup at that point." She exhaled. "Be careful. If they think you have the whole treasure, or know where it is, there's nothing they won't do. You need to make them think that you stumbled upon just this one piece."

The man twisted a pencil in his fingers.

"Don't worry about me," he said. "But you raise a good point. Where is the rest of it?"

Alexandra's eyes flashed.

"Don't even think about it."

"Me? Never, we go back too far," he said. "But let me give you a piece of advice. Keep your mouth shut after you leave here. I'm talking about the kind of shut where you don't even open it to breathe. You've been in archeology a long time. You think you know how things work. But trust me, you've always been in the clean part of the dirt. There's a whole other world out there that you don't ever want to know about."

78

Day Eight—July 19
Monday Morning

———————

The caveman's girlfriend, Chantal Thomas, turned out to be an intellectual property attorney in Bertrand, Roux & Blanc, Ltd., which was a mega law firm that occupied three floors of the ultra-chic EDF Tower in La Defense. Durand took a shady spot outside the building shortly before the lunch hour, pulled up a wireless Internet connection, and worked the handheld on a different case while he waited for the woman to emerge.

She didn't for quite some time but eventually did.

Patience.

That's what this game was about.

Patience.

Durand hoped that she would meet the caveman for lunch. Then Durand would follow him. But she did even better than that. She came out of the building with the caveman at her side.

Not arm in arm.

Not like lovers.

More as professionals.

Unlike yesterday, the man was now dressed to impress in a wool-blend suit, a red power-tie and expensive Italian shoes.

He looked like a lawyer.

He looked even less now than the man Durand saw through the door crack.

Did he work at the same law firm as the woman?

Was he her boss?

That would explain the beauty-and-the-beast mystery.

Durand followed them to an expensive restaurant.

They disappeared inside.

He found a bench, opened the handheld, logged onto the firm's website and went through the attorney biographies. Luckily they had photographs. One of those photographs turned out to belong to the caveman.

Paul Sabater.

That was his name.

Paul Sabater.

Durand frowned.

An important lawyer wouldn't be running around at night shooting lowlifes in the head.

Dead end.

Time wasted.

Time he could have spent better on the taxi driver, Anton Fornier, or his brother, Serge.

From La Defense he went to the Laughing Hat Cafe, got a sidewalk table in Prarie's section and ordered a sandwich and wine. She bent in and whispered, "Would you like that with a side of spanking?"

He chuckled.

"Maybe later."

She rubbed her ass suggestively and said, "There's no extra charge."

He tilted his head.

"Can I get that to go, for later?"

"Oui."

"In that case, you talked me into it."

Five minutes later, his cell phone rang and the voice of Emmanuelle from Blue Moon came through. "How's it going?" she asked, referring to Sharla DePaglia, the wild beauty from Rome who got suffocated.

"Believe it or not, I was working on it this morning," he said. "I think I may be onto something, but I don't want to get ahead of myself."

"Exciting," she said.

"We'll see," he said.

She said, "The phone number I gave you before has been retired. Here's the new one—"

From the café, he swung by the houseboat and found it just as quiet and lifeless as last night. Had the snakes done their job? He sat down, closed his eyes and pulled up an image of the woman stretched out on the rack at De Luna with her wonderful tattoo, being felt up and tickled by strangers.

The image made his cock tighten against his pants.

He put a hand in his lap and applied downward pressure, nothing anyone would notice but feeling so good.

He needed his dick sucked.

For a brief moment, he thought about paying a visit to the blond hooker down at Verdant Park, but then realized that part of his life was over.

79

Teffinger loved Monday mornings because that's when he had the whole week ahead of him. He usually jogged but didn't today because he needed his strength for the desert, if they ended up there. He did, however, surprise Fallon when she stepped out of the shower by throwing her on the mattress and taking her.

"God, Teffinger, you just used up all my energy for the whole day," she said afterwards.

He patted himself on the back.

"I need coffee."

Luckily, the hotel had heard of the stuff and, in fact, had a truckload on hand, which was just about the right amount. As they woke up, Fallon called Targaux and asked, "Can you do something for me?"

What?

She explained.

"Why didn't you do that before you left?"

"Because I didn't think of it," she said. "In fact, I didn't even think of it now, Teffinger did. By the way, our plane crashed yesterday."

"Yeah, right."

"Will you do it?"

He grunted.

"Okay, but I'm making a sour face right now, just for the record."

A half hour later he called back.

It turned out that Deja Lafayette had two credit cards. One had been used all over Luxor the last couple of days, including the Golden Palace Hotel on Television Street.

She told Teffinger.

He looked at his watch.

"Let's see if we can catch her before she heads out."

The Golden Palace turned out to be a 3-star budget hotel on a main street near the west bank, a stone's throw from the train station. Deja Lafayette wasn't there, naturally, because that's how Teffinger's life worked. But the receptionist said the women hadn't checked out, so they must be around somewhere.

"Women?"

"Right."

"As in more than one?"

"Right. Deja Lafayette and Alexandra Reed."

Fallon looked at Teffinger, made a sour face and said, "He's going to kill me."

Then she called Targaux again.

"Is this some kind of a plan to make me think that you two aren't in a hot tub drinking wine?" he asked. "Because if it is, it's not working."

She grinned.

"Alexandra Reed," she said. "She's someone rooming down

here with Deja Lafayette. It would be nice if I knew who she was."

Targaux grunted and called back fifteen minutes later with a lot more information than Fallon expected. Teffinger drank coffee and watched as she spoke, wondering if he could learn to speak French. She hung up and said, "Alexandra Reed is an archeologist. She lived in Cairo until three years ago, then moved to Paris."

Teffinger cocked his head.

"So she knows the turf around here."

"Right."

"Maybe she's the 10-year-old Alexandra in the 18-year-old notes."

80

Day Eight—July 19
Monday Afternoon

---

maury posted photos of the coin on his website, spent an hour making long distance telephone calls, some of them very long distance, and then grinned at the women. "Your bait is in the trap. Now we get drunk."

He took them to a belly-dance bar, set them on barstools and filled their tummies with wine.

The lighting was dim.

The air conditioning was heaven.

The music was Middle Eastern, sensual and erotic.

The bartender—a curvy brunette named Andrea—wore a long-sleeve white blouse tied just below her breasts, showcasing a very nice stomach.

The dancers all knew Amaury.

They crowded around, gyrated up-close-and-personal, and let him buy them shots. He stayed at Deja's side and every so often turned and kissed her on the mouth. She stopped resisting after the first few times and began to wonder what he was like in bed.

"Your kissing is improving," he told her.

"Yours too."

He grinned.

Ten minutes later he took her by the hand and said, "I want to show you something."

"Yeah? What?"

He led her to a back storage room, stood her against the wall, and flicked off the lights. The world turned blacker than black. Then he kneeled before her, unbuttoned her shorts and slid them down.

She bit her lip, deciding, and stepped out of them.

When she got back to the barstool a half hour later, Alexandra handed her a fresh glass of wine and said, "Well, it looks like you're enjoying Cairo."

"Yeah, it's bigger than I thought."

Alexandra rolled her eyes.

"Bad, even for you."

"Bad but accurate." She took a sip of wine. "Or did you already know that?"

Alexandra frowned.

"Actually I didn't, not that I didn't want to at one point in time," she said. "Look, we need to talk about something. You have the right to know what's going on."

"You mean about Amaury?"

No.

She didn't.

"Forget about him for a minute," Alexandra said. "I wanted to tell you what I'm about to tell you a hundred different times, but we were still in the middle of things. Now we're not. Now we're at the end of things and you have a right to know the truth. I've lied to you about a lot of things. I've lied to you all along, from the very beginning. I'm sorry."

Deja set the glass down and studied Alexandra.

"What the hell are you talking about?"

"Okay, it goes like this," Alexandra said. "I have a friend named Michelle Berri, an archeology friend—I let her tag along on some of my projects. Anyway, that's not the point. The point is that a week ago, I got a strange phone call from a man who said he had abducted Michelle. He said he'd kill her unless I did exactly what he said."

"This is a joke, right?"

"No. He also said that he killed Michelle's roommate, just so I'd know he was serious. He said he gouged her eyes out and then stuck them in backwards."

"Was that true?"

Alexandra nodded.

"Yes."

"I called Michelle right away but didn't get an answer," Alexandra said. "The next day, there was an article in the newspaper. Michelle's roommate—a woman named Margaux Simon—had been found dead in her home. The police were treating it as a homicide. The article also reported that Michelle Berri was missing." She exhaled. "There was nothing in the article about Margaux's eyes being gouged out, but I figured the police wouldn't release that kind of detail anyway."

So he was telling the truth.

Absolutely.

"How terrible," Deja said.

Alexandra nodded.

"It gets worse," she said. "The man called me the next day and let me talk to Michelle briefly, just so I knew she was alive and really was in his control. Then he told me what I needed to do. He asked me if I knew about the tomb recently discovered in the Valley of the Kings and about the missing treasure."

"So he knew you were an archeologist," Deja said.

Right.

Exactly.

"That's why he targeted me," Alexandra said. "Anyway, I told him I was aware of it. He said that he had hired Remy Lafayette—your uncle—to find that treasure. Remy had been working on the project for three months and recently told the man he believed he knew where it was. There was a map. The man wasn't sure if the map was something Remy found, like an original document, or whether it was something he drew himself, based on his investigation. Anyway, the man came to Paris to meet with Remy about what to do next."

Alexandra swallowed.

"When he got there," she added, "he found Remy dead. All his files were gone."

"So this man wasn't the one who killed Remy," Deja said.

No.

Not according to him, anyway.

He said it was probably looters who somehow heard through the grapevine that Remy had a map.

They went to get it from him.

It didn't work out very good for anyone.

"Anyway," Alexandra said, "He wanted me to pick up where Remy left off. He wanted me to find the map or find the treasure. Then he'd let Michelle go."

Deja ran her hands through her hair.

"Why didn't he just hire you like he did with Remy?"

Alexandra grunted.

"Funny you should ask, because I actually questioned him

about that," she said. "He told me I'd never go for it because he was going to keep the treasure. It wouldn't end up in a museum."

Deja cocked her head.

"Is that the deal he had with Remy?"

Alexandra shrugged.

She didn't know.

"So what did you do?" Deja asked.

"You actually know most of it," Alexandra said. "The first thing I did was go to your apartment to see if you knew anything about the map or maybe even had a copy of it by chance. You remember that day."

Deja did—coming home after work to find the place torn apart.

"So you're the one who searched my apartment?"

"No," she said. "I would have but the looters got to it first. But I did lie to you. I told you I was working for the Egyptian government, which I wasn't. I had to have some kind of a reason to get you to help me find the map and that's the best story I could come up with."

"Why didn't you just tell me the truth?"

"Lots of reasons," Alexandra said. "Primarily because the man swore he'd kill Michelle if I told a single soul what was going on. But beyond that, I didn't know you yet. I didn't know if you'd believe me or not. And if you did believe me, I didn't know if you'd work with me or just report the whole thing to the police. If you had done that, Michelle would be dead right now, I know that for a fact." She cocked her head. "What would you have done, in hindsight?"

Deja thought about it.

She didn't know.

It was a moot point anyway.

"You know what happened after that," Alexandra said. "We broke into Remy's place. I was hoping that something would spark in your mind as to where he might hide things, but nothing did. We went to my place. The looters showed up. My guess is that they had been staking out Remy's house, saw us searching around, speculated that we might have found the map, and followed us. That night one of them broke in. You ended up shooting him. You remember that, I suppose."

Deja nodded.

Only too well.

"Here's the bottom line," Alexandra said. "We found the treasure. I've already contacted the man and told him. He let me talk to Michelle to verify she's still alive. The man is coming to Luxor tonight. He's going to bring Michelle. We're going to make the exchange. I don't want you anywhere around when that happens."

"But—"

"There are no buts," Alexandra said. "I'm not going to put you at risk and that's all there is to it. Stay here in Cairo and wait for me. You'll be safe with Amaury. And speaking of Amaury, don't tell him a word of this. He needs to stay focused on finding the looters."

Alexandra looked at her watch.

"I need to get to the airport."

81

Day Eight—July 19
Monday Afternoon

---

urand threw a rock into the Seine, took one more look at the lifeless houseboat and checked his watch. It was time to head to the hideaway where Michelle Berri was being kept. Unlike Saturday night, when he came here with Prarie after dark and parked at the edge of the field, this time he drove directly to the house and parked the car at the far end of the long dirt driveway, out of sight behind vegetation.

The nearest house was fifty or sixty meters away.

He put on latex gloves, entered through the back door and pulled a ski mask over his face. Then he walked downstairs to the basement, knocked on a steel door and said, "Michelle, put your blindfold on. Do you hear me?"

Yes.

Durand waited, giving her time.

He knew she was obeying because if she ever saw anyone's face, she would have to die.

"It's on," she said.

"Sit on the bed and put your hands on your head," he said.

He opened the door and stepped in.

She was positioned as she should be.

He checked her blindfold, found it secure, pulled his ski mask off and scratched the itch off his face.

There.

Better.

He could breathe again.

She was a nice girl, twenty-four, short brown hair, five-foot-three, strong legs, tiny chest and, best of all, obedient. She hadn't given Durand a speck of trouble.

"This is the day you've been waiting for," he said. "You're going to be released."

He expected her to smile but she didn't.

She was processing the information.

"You're messing with me."

"I'm not," he said. "Let me tell you how it's going to work. You're going to get into the trunk of my car. I'm going to drive to the airport. You're going to board a private jet."

"A private jet?"

Yes.

That's right.

"You're going to fly to Luxor, Egypt. That's where you'll be released."

"Luxor? Why Luxor?"

"It's a long story," Durand said. "Here's the important thing. You need to cooperate every single step of the way. If you do, then everything will turn out fine. If you don't, things will go badly. You've come this far. Don't screw it up now. Do you understand?"

Yes.

She did.

"Behave yourself and you'll be free by midnight," he said.

She would behave

She promised.

"I like you better than the other man who was taking care of me," she said. "He was mean."

"He died in a car crash," Durand said.

"Good. I hope he suffered."

82

Day Eight—July 19
Monday

———————

The two women didn't show up at their hotel room all day long. Teffinger and Fallon knew that and knew it well, because they staked it out hour after agonizingly hot hour.

Waiting.

Sweating.

Pacing.

Deja Lafayette had answers.

Maybe Alexandra Reed did too.

They were the connection to the killer.

The day turned to twilight, the twilight turned to night, and the night turned to a pitch-black sky with a moon inching across it.

Teffinger and Fallon stayed where they were.

"I feel like one of those guys at a slot machine who's been loosing money all day," Teffinger said. "I can't get up and walk away, because as soon as I do, some slob's going to sit down and hit the jackpot on the first pull."

Fallon flicked hair out of her eyes.

"That's the way my life works too," she said. "It's almost like there's someone up there screwing with me."

Teffinger nodded.

Exactly.

Then something weird happened.

A man and woman screeched a car to a stop in front of the hotel and ran inside.

"Come on," Teffinger said.

By the time Teffinger and Fallon got to the entrance, the man and woman were running out of the hotel, as if they had come to see if someone was there and got a negative. "Hey, hold on," Teffinger said.

The man pushed by.

"No time, buddy."

Teffinger snagged the woman's arm and yanked her to a stop.

"Are you Deja Lafayette?"

The woman stared as if trying to figure out if she knew him.

"Maybe," she said. "Who are you?"

They talked.

Fast.

Heated.

And Teffinger found out something he wouldn't have expected in a million years—Michelle Berri was alive and was supposed to be exchanged for the treasure.

Tonight, as they spoke.

"He won't give her up until he's actually seen the treasure and verified it's not a trick," Teffinger said. "That's where they are. At the treasure."

No kidding.

Let's go.

They took the car as far as the roads let them into the Valley of the Kings and then trotted west on foot with the woman, Deja Lafayette, leading the way. She provided more and more of the story as they went.

Teffinger's heart raced.

Somewhere out there in the blackness was the man who killed Amanda Peterson and Tracy White.

And took Michelle Berri.

"Make no mistake," Teffinger said. "He's going to kill them both. He has to. There are too many ways for things to go wrong if they stay alive."

"We already know that," the man said.

Teffinger grunted.

"What's your name, buddy?"

"Amaury."

"Amaury?"

"Right."

"Nice to meet you, Amaury."

"Likewise, my friend."

"We're getting close," Deja said. "Another couple hundred meters."

They slowed to a walk, got as quiet as they could and closed in.

The moonlight was faint, but was strong enough for Teffinger to see four men climbing up the face of the mountain. Two more were at the base. One of them held a rifle and paced. The other held a pistol and stood behind two women who were kneeling on the ground with their hands on their heads. No doubt Alexandra Reed and Michelle Berri.

Teffinger always thought the man would be alone.

He now realized how stupid that had been.

He would want to get the treasure out of there tonight, which would take more muscle than one man had.

So which one was the killer?

Probably one of the guys climbing up.

He'd want to see the treasure with his own eyes.

Probably the top guy.

Teffinger focused on him. He looked big and strong and had long hair. He moved with agility.

Yeah.

You're him.

Now what?

Fallon tugged at his arm. "We're out of time," she said. "As soon as he verifies the treasure's there, he's going to give the orders to shoot."

83

Day Eight—July 19
Monday Night

———————————

S omeone shouted from above, "It's here, just like she said. Go ahead and do it." The man standing behind the two women stepped closer, released the safety and pointed the barrel at the back of a head.

"I'm sorry," he said. "Go ahead and take a second to make your peace."

Teffinger charged and lunged through the air.

Not too soon this time.

Not like at the houseboat.

The man landed under him and Teffinger immediately pummeled his head with every ounce of strength he had and didn't stop until the man went limp.

He didn't know what Amaury did to the man with the rifle but he was on the ground motionless, maybe dead.

No shouts or questions came from above.

"Get the women back to Luxor," Teffinger told Amaury.

They left.

Amaury.

Alexandra Reed.

Deja Lafayette.

And Michelle Berri.

Fallon was holding the rifle when Teffinger turned to her. He scouted around until he found the pistol and stuffed it in his belt.

"Now what?" Fallon asked.

"I'm going to go up and send them down one at a time," he said. "Make them lay on the ground face down with their hands out. If they move, shoot them."

"Why don't we just wait for them to come down? We have them trapped—"

"Not necessarily," Teffinger said. "They might go up once they find out we're here."

Teffinger headed up.

The face was steeper and trickier than it looked. Coming back down would be a problem, a serious problem. He'd worry about that when the time came. He was almost to the cave when something bad happened.

The gun slipped out of his belt and dropped into the blackness below.

It bounced off the rocks and landed with a thud.

His instinct was to climb down and get it. But the mountain was darker below him and almost impossible to read. He pictured himself falling and breaking his back.

He headed up.

The mouth of the cave was narrow, not much wider than his shoulders. He got on his stomach and muscled halfway through. Inside, he heard voices and saw flickers of light from deeper inside. He squirmed all the way in and stood up.

Then someone shouted, "Snakes!"

Almost immediately, gunfire erupted.

Explosions of light came from inside the cave, around a corner, maybe two corners. He saw something move, five steps away, on the ground.

Bang!

Bang!

"There's a whole nest!" someone shouted.

Bang!

Bang!

Bang, bang, bang!

Bang!

Teffinger turned to get out but suddenly a man ran his way, shining a flashlight on the ground and shooting snakes. His bullets ran out and he threw the gun at the closest one. He missed. Seconds later he screamed, grabbed his leg and dropped to the ground. The flashlight landed next to his face and lit it up as he died.

Teffinger froze.

He didn't move a muscle.

He didn't know where they were or how many there were.

More shots came from deeper inside.

Bang!

Bang!

Bang!

Then the bullets ran out and the shooting stopped. Everything got quiet but flashlights still flickered. Teffinger knew he had to get out and get out now, but he didn't have the guts to get down on his stomach. He stepped carefully over to the flashlight, slowly reached down and picked it up.

Then he frantically swept the area.

No snakes.

Where did they go?

Someone in the other room shouted, "I'm bit!" Then someone else screamed. Suddenly a man ran around the corner and headed for the mouth of the cave. Teffinger turned his light on the man's face and saw fear like he had never seen before.

It was the big man.

The strong man.

The one with the long hair.

The killer.

"Get out of my way!" he said.

Then he dropped to his stomach and started to crawl out. Teffinger grabbed his legs and pulled him back. The man stood up and swung at Teffinger's face. But he wasn't fast enough. Teffinger hit him first.

Hard.

On the nose.

Blood splattered.

He stumbled and fell onto this back.

Teffinger got on him and pounded his face.

Movement caught his peripheral vision.

Snakes.

Three snakes.

Coming at them.

On the ground behind the man's head.

Teffinger jumped up at the last second and stepped back until the wall stopped him. The flashlights were on the ground. None of them pointed directly at the man but they gave off enough light to show three snakes sinking their fangs into his face.

Vomit shot into Teffinger's mouth.

He swallowed it.

The man twisted in agony for a few moments and then grew silent. The only sounds left in the world were the rustling of snakes on the ground and the beating of Teffinger's own heart.

Ba boom.

Ba boom.

Ba boom.

84

Day Nine—July 20
Tuesday

Tuesday morning, after debriefing the Luxor police, Teffinger and Fallon boarded a train for Cairo. It was hot and stuffy but rolled through spectacular scenery and couldn't drop out of the sky. The man with the long hair turned out to be Nicholas Ringer from Nice, France—a shipbuilder, a very rich shipbuilder to be precise, a very rich shipbuilder who wanted to possess the greatest treasure on the face of the earth to be even more precise. Teffinger had a bad feeling about the man ever since last night because he was anything but a caveman.

Tuesday afternoon, Targaux called.

Teffinger didn't think the news would be good.

He was right.

It wasn't.

Ringer was in Amsterdam during the entire week when Amanda Peterson got her eyes gouged out in Denver. There was no question about it. Several disinterested witnesses placed him there, not to mention credit card receipts, cell phone records and all the other circumstantial evidence, meaning he didn't kill Amanda Peterson.

Damn it.

"Back to square one," Teffinger said.

Fallon patted his hand.

"I don't get it," he said. "He gouged out Tracy White's eyes as an exact copycat of what someone did to a different woman thousands of miles away a year earlier. It doesn't make sense."

Fallon agreed but had no brilliant ideas.

"In hindsight, all he really wanted to do was kidnap Michelle Berri, so he could put pressure on Alexandra to make her use her archeological skills to either find the map or find the treasure," Teffinger said. "I don't see why he even needed to kill Tracy White at all, much less in such a weird way."

"Maybe she came home while he was inside, waiting to abduct Michelle," Fallon said. "Or maybe he did it to put a sufficient scare on Alexandra so she'd take him seriously. Who knows?"

Right.

Who knows?

Ringer knows, but he wasn't talking.

"To me, just taking Michelle would be enough to get Alexandra to jump through hoops," Teffinger said. "Maybe killing the roommate gave him a little more credibility, but not much, especially when compared to the risk."

"Then maybe Michelle came home at the wrong time, like I said."

"Right, but if he had to kill her, why gouge out her eyes?" Teffinger ran his fingers through his hair. "I just don't get it. I feel further away from solving this case now than I did at the beginning."

Fallon tilted her head.

"That's called negative investigation."

"Negative investigation, huh?"

"Right."

"Maybe I'll teach that at the university someday," he said. "Negative investigation. No one does it better than me, that's for sure."

85

Day Ten—July 21
Wednesday

———

Teffinger and Fallon didn't land in Paris until after midnight, then took a cab to the houseboat and fell into bed too exhausted to make love.

The wind kicked up.

The Seine got choppy and lapped against the hull.

Teffinger had too much caffeine pumping through his nervous system and tossed from side to side to prove it.

Then something happened.

A light flickered.

Teffinger opened his eyes and focused.

Nothing.

No light.

He concentrated harder.

Nothing.

He turned on his side, fluffed the pillow under his head and closed his eyes. He was almost asleep when it happened again; a flicker of light. He opened his eyes and saw it this time.

A flashlight was coming down the steps.

Before he could get out of bed, the light entered the room and shined in his eyes.

"Don't move!" someone said.

Teffinger knew he should obey.

Don't move!

Stay calm!

Bide your time!

But something snapped in his brain and made him charge. A heartbeat later, white-hot pain came from his upper chest.

From a knife.

Teffinger swung his fists.

They landed but not squarely.

Then another pain came, deeper and more intense, so agonizing that he stepped back. His foot caught on something and he fell onto his back.

Then the man was on top of him.

And said, "Die asshole!"

Teffinger swung, missed, and then shielded his face with his arms.

Pop! Pop! Pop!

Gunfire.

Coming from Fallon.

The man's muscles lost their intensity.

Then he made a terrible noise and fell.

His face landed on Teffinger's and felt like bloody meat.

Fallon turned on the lights and Teffinger muscled out from under the body. All three bullets landed in the man's head, but there was enough of it left to make out the face.

It wasn't a caveman.

Teffinger had seen the man somewhere before but couldn't place it. Then it came to him. This was the man who had been sitting on the bench down the walkway, working on his laptop—the one Teffinger walked over to and asked if he'd seen anyone suspicious hanging around the boat.

Suddenly a motion caught his eye.

Something was coming down the steps.

A rattlesnake.

Then another one.

Two rattlesnakes.

86

Day Ten—July 21
Wednesday

Teffinger threw a blanket over the snakes and got Fallon safely upstairs, then off the boat and onto the walkway, where he collapsed. Fallon put pressure on his wounds and called an ambulance.

Sirens and flashing lights showed up three minutes later.

Teffinger got a frightening ride to the hospital where he was treated for two stabs to the upper chest, both of which were deep but missed the heart.

"Probably because you don't have one," Fallon said.

Daylight was just starting to break over Paris when they got back to the boat and found Targaux processing the scene.

He gave Fallon a long hug and said, "You okay?"

She nodded.

Yes.

She was.

A woman walked off the boat carrying a bag. "Got two of them," she said, referring to snakes. "There could be more though, so we better fumigate."

Teffinger and Fallon gave their statements.

Fallon had never seen the man before.

She had no idea who he was.

Suddenly Teffinger needed coffee, needed it bad and needed it now.

While Targaux processed the scene, Teffinger and Fallon walked down the street to drink coffee and eat croissants at a sidewalk cafe under a sun that didn't bake them to death on impact.

So nice.

"The only thing I can figure is that this is fallout from our bait plan," Teffinger said. "The caveman is still trying to get you. Only now he's shy because I almost caught him once. My guess is that he hired the dead guy to take you out."

He looked at her for a reaction but she looked vacant and shrugged.

"That makes sense," she said. "But I don't know. It's too complicated."

Teffinger frowned. "That bait plan was the worst idea I ever had. If I could go back in time and change one thing, that would be it." He hesitated, then took her hand and said, "There's probably never going to be a perfect time to say this, so I'm going to just get it out in the open. I know we've only known each other a week, but I don't ever want to wake up in the morning and not find you next to me. I like Paris. I like you. So I'm thinking I should move here."

She looked stunned.

Then her eyes got moist and she squeezed his hand.

"I really wish you hadn't said that," she said.

"Why, you don't want me to?"

"No, I do, more than anything," she said. "I feel the same way, more even."

"So what's the problem? I don't get it—"

"The problem is that I always pictured you going back to Denver," she said. "And when you did, that meant I wouldn't have to tell you certain things."

Teffinger wrinkled his brow.

"I'm not following."

"I couldn't let you move to Paris unless I gave you full disclosure," she said.

"What does that mean?"

"It means I haven't been completely honest with you about a few things."

She was on the verge of tears.

Teffinger put 20 euros on the table, grabbed Fallon around the waist and headed for somewhere private. They walked for ten minutes and ended up sitting on a bench by Notre Dame.

"Now talk to me," he said. "What the hell's going on?"

"Okay, but just remember, I'm not perfect and never said I was," she said. "Let me start at the beginning. About a year ago, I was out with some friends doing some clubbing, down at Rex, actually."

Rex?

That's where the caveman DJ worked.

"Right, but this isn't about him," she said. "I was at the bar minding my own business when a woman walked over and kissed me on the lips like I was her love slave. I was just about to slap her when I looked into her eyes. That was my big mistake. She wasn't just striking, she was beyond description, raw and compelling and mysterious. Maybe it was the alcohol or the music or the lighting or a time in my life where I was curious, but I was totally hypnotized. I wanted her. I wanted her badly, right from the very first second."

Teffinger grinned.

"I totally understand," he said. "And for your information, so far I'm liking this story."

She punched him on the arm.

"You would," she said. "Anyway, she took me to the dance floor and got me hot. She kissed me and felt me up and grinded on me. People stared and we didn't care. Then she took me to the ladies room. We went into a stall and she pulled out a small bottle of cocaine and a little spoon. She took a sniff. Then I did. That was the first time I'd ever done that."

"Do you still—?"

She shook her head.

No.

That was the one and only time.

"But it got me in trouble," she said. "Big trouble."

"How?"

"Well, at that point, I wouldn't have left this woman's side if she was falling off the edge of the earth," Fallon said. "Then she got a phone call. She talked in private for a second, hung up and said she had to go."

"Go where?"

"To do a gig," Fallon said.

"What kind of gig?"

"A sex gig," Fallon said. "It turned out that she was a high-priced escort who just started working for a group called Blue Moon, which I had never heard of at the time. This was going to be a bondage gig that would last an hour or two. She said she'd come back afterwards but I knew she wouldn't. Then I did something stupid and told her to take me with her. She said fine and off we went."

Teffinger shook his head.

"What does all this have to do with me moving to Paris?"

"I'm getting there," Fallon said. "Just hold on. Anyway, we ended up going to a building that was being renovated. A man met us there. He seemed nice. He told the other woman that he wanted to put her in a standing spread-eagle position, feel her up and vibrate her. He wasn't into pain or whipping or anything like that. The other woman said fine and he strung her up. Then she looked at me and said, Come on and join us. The man looked at me. And said, Yeah, you want to?"

"What'd you say?"

"I said fine and he strung me up, face to face with this incredibly beautiful woman," Fallon said. "He tied a rope around our waists so that our stomachs stayed together. Our breasts pressed against each other. We were totally naked. Then he started to vibrate the woman between the legs and finger me at the same time."

"Sounds like fun," Teffinger said.

"It was. Then it got ugly—very ugly."

"Why? What happened?"

"He said we were going to notch it up a little, and he put ball gags in our mouths. At first it freaked me out, but they were breathable and didn't restrict my airflow, they just kept us from calling out. Then he went back to teasing us. Everything was fine. Then he put a plastic bag around the other woman's head and sealed it around her neck with duct tape. She suffocated to death, right in front of me. Then he said, *Your turn.*"

She exhaled.

"I pulled at the ropes as hard as I could but it did no good," Fallon said. "He was just about to put a bag over my head when someone broke a window and shouted something. The man ran away."

She looked at Teffinger.

"I suppose you figured out the other woman's name by now," she said.

He had.

He had indeed.

Sharla DePaglia.

"Right," she said. "From there, everything went downhill."

87

Day Ten—July 21
Wednesday

———————

The man who broke the window turned out to be someone from Blue Moon who came over to be sure everything was okay," Fallon said. "He cut me down and took me to a house in the Luxembourg Quarter. I met with a woman named Emmanuelle and told her what happened. Then she took me home. Sharla DePaglia was found the next morning when the construction crew showed up. Then the weirdest thing in the world happened."

"What?"

"Targaux responded and asked me to come with him," Fallon said. "That's when I made my big mistake. I should have told him about my involvement right then and there. I should have told him that I was a witness and could identify the killer. I should have told him I had a conflict of interest."

Teffinger nodded.

True.

That would be the right thing to do.

"But I didn't tell him," Fallon said. "I was scared. I was

scared of what he'd think. I was scared of getting fired. I was scared of being ridiculed. So I stayed quiet as if I didn't know a thing."

Teffinger frowned.

"That was wrong."

She sighed.

She knew that.

She knew that a hundred times over.

"Then, out of the blue, Targaux assigns the case to me," Fallon said. "It was my very first case as the lead detective."

"That's a strange turn of events," Teffinger said.

She nodded.

"In a way, it was the best thing and the worst thing that could have happened," Fallon said. "It was the best thing because I actually knew what the killer looked like and knew what happened. All I had to do was find him. But it was the worst thing, too, because I wouldn't be able to arrest him once I found him. I couldn't arrest him because he'd tell everyone I was actually the other woman. I couldn't let that happen, not only because it was true, but because I'd also kept quiet and hadn't disclosed it when I should have."

Teffinger raised an eyebrow.

"That's quite a dilemma," he said. "But if that's your full disclosure—that you got attracted to another woman, or took cocaine, or kept quiet when you should have talked—I don't really care about any of those things. The not-talking part was a bad decision, but I could see how it could happen."

She shook her head.

"No, that's not the disclosure," she said.

It isn't?

No.

There's more.

"It gets worse," she said.

"I wanted more than anything in the world to bring this guy down," Fallon said, "not only because of what he did to Sharla DePaglia right in front of my face, but because I knew he'd kill me if he ever found out who I was."

"Because you could identify him," Teffinger said.

She nodded.

Exactly.

"I knew he was into bondage, so I started frequenting the places where he might show up, on the hopes of bumping into him," she said. "I always wore a disguise. I put in more hours than you can believe, all on my own time. It was inevitable that sooner or later our paths would cross. I got more and more concerned about what to do once that happened."

"You're back to your Catch-22," Teffinger said.

Yes.

The dreaded Catch-22.

"Meanwhile," Fallon said, "I was staying in contact with Emmanuelle at Blue Moon. One day she proposed a very simple solution. All I had to do was find out who the guy was and let her know. She'd hire a hitman to kill him."

Teffinger frowned.

Fallon must have read the look on his face because she said, "I know, the whole idea was wrong, but at the same time it was so right. The guy would end up dead, as he needed to be, and my secret would forever stay a secret. So, with that plan in mind, I continued to frequent the bondage haunts on the hopes of running into the guy and feeding his name to Emmanuelle."

She paused and exhaled.

"Do you hate me yet?"

Teffinger squeezed her hand.

"Of course not.

She swallowed.

"It gets worse."

"There's an underground club in the Latin Quarter called De Luna," Fallon said. "Every two months, they have a fetish night. They actually tie up women, show bondage movies, stuff like that. It's a huge event. Several hundred people show up. They dress in leather and chains and get drunk."

Really?

Teffinger had no idea.

"Anyway," Fallon said, "they had a fetish night set for last Monday."

"You mean the day I came to Paris?"

Right.

Then.

"You and I had talked about using me for bait earlier that day," Fallon said. "You ended up staying at the houseboat that night. I got up, after you went to sleep, and went to De Luna as part of my continuing efforts to find the guy."

Teffinger remembered waking up in the middle of the night.

Fallon wasn't there.

The next day he asked where she was.

She said she couldn't sleep and took a walk.

"I had to say that," she said, "because if I told you I went to a bar, then I'd have to explain the whole thing."

"I understand," Teffinger said.

"At the club," Fallon said, "something happened that hadn't happened in a whole year. I actually saw the guy."

"You did?"

She nodded.

Yes.

"There was a problem, though," she said. "I wasn't positive it was him. I was pretty sure it was him—more than 95 percent—but I wasn't absolutely positive. It had been a year since I'd seen him and I was on cocaine at the time. And his face was ordinary. There wasn't anything about it that really stood out. So, I didn't know what to do."

"So what did you do?"

"Well, at first I thought about watching him from a distance and then trying to follow him after he left the club," she said. "With any luck, I could get a license plate number or something to tell me who he was."

"And?"

"And then I realized something," she said. "Even if I succeeded, and found out his name and where he lived and everything else, I still wouldn't be positive he was the one. I couldn't call Emmanuelle, and have her put a hitman on the guy, without knowing for sure that he was the right person."

Teffinger picked up a twig and broke it.

He understood.

"Plus," Fallon said, "by that time I had totally reevaluated the whole hitman thing. As convenient as it would have been, I was beginning to get more and more reluctant to be a party to it, even though it would solve all my problems."

"Well, that's good to hear."

"Thank you," she said.

"So what did you do?"

"I did something I wish I hadn't," she said.

"What does that mean?"

"It means you might hate me after I tell you the last part."

Teffinger doubted that but said, "So tell me."

She diverted her eyes. "Before I tell you the last part, I want to tell you something else first. I love you. I have from the first moment I saw you. I think you already know that."

Teffinger nodded.

He did but it was still nice to hear.

"That's all that matters," he said.

"You better hear the rest of the story before you say that," Fallon said.

She exhaled.

Okay, here goes.

"Last Monday night, at De Luna, I made a split-second decision," she said. "I figured that the only way I'd know for sure if this man was in fact the right one, was to let him see me. If he was in fact the right man, he'd follow me and try to kill me. If he wasn't, he wouldn't. There was a woman stretched out on a rack and people were paying 5 euros to feel her up and tickle her. This guy was there watching."

Okay.

So what happened?

"When she got off, I got on," Fallon said. "They stretched me out. I told the guy who was taking the money for the prior woman to keep doing what he was doing. I told him he could keep all the money. He was fine with that, of course. I also told him to put a blindfold on me. The reason I did that was so that this guy would feel safe taking a good long look at me. In any event, if he was the right one, he'd know me by my tattoo. To make a long story short, I spent some time on the rack. Then I got dressed and left the club."

"So now you were bait," Teffinger said.

Right.

Bait.

"I walked back to the houseboat so he'd be able to follow me if he wanted," she said. "The way I pictured it in my mind, if he was in fact the killer, he'd come to get me. I would kill him and you'd be my witness that it was self defense. That would solve all my problems. My secret would be safe. I wouldn't have to participate in a hitman scheme. I'd know that he was the right person. And he'd be justifiably killed."

"I lied to you," she said. "I told you that I gave my name to someone pretending to be from INTERPOL who wanted to know who the page 5 witness was. You thought that the bait plan that you and I talked about was all set and in place. Actually, that whole thing was a lie. I made the whole thing up. The reason I did that was so you'd be watching your back, and mine. I didn't want the guy to show up to kill me and then blindside you when you didn't suspect it. Also, deep down, I hoped that you'd kill him."

Teffinger raked his hair with his fingers.

It immediately flopped back down.

"The dead man in the bedroom of my boat is the man from De Luna," Fallon said. "Now I know for sure that he's the one who killed Sharla DePaglia."

"So that case is solved," Teffinger said.

"Solved is the wrong word," Fallon said. "Resolved is the better word."

Teffinger nodded.

Right.

Resolved.

Over.

Done.

"In hindsight," Fallon said, "he was no doubt the man you lunged at. Actually, it was a good thing he escaped, because if you had captured him alive, I would have been screwed."

Teffinger retreated in thought.

He said, "Do you remember when we got back to the boat a couple of days ago and found that burlap bag on the deck? The one you thought was trash that someone had tossed on board?"

Yes.

She remembered.

"I'll bet the snakes were in there," Teffinger said. "I can see him walking by and nonchalantly tossing it onboard. The snakes would crawl out and you'd eventually bump into them. That was a pretty good plan, actually, because he'd already had a close encounter with me. So he came up with a way to kill you without even being there."

She squeezed his hand.

"If that's true, then we spent a lot of time on the boat with those things right there somewhere," she said.

True.

"We were lucky," Teffinger said. "When you didn't die, he must have figured the snakes left. Then he got impatient and decided to get it over with."

Fallon nodded.

"That's my disclosure," she said. "You got stabbed twice and almost got killed thanks to me."

"All to get your guy," Teffinger said.

She nodded.

Right.

"That's the first person you killed," Teffinger said. "How does it feel?"

Silence.

Then she said, "It feels like Sharla DePaglia is finally at

peace."

Her eyes got moist and she laid her head on his arm.

"So do you still want to move to Paris?"

Teffinger put his arm around her and squeezed.

"Are you done? Or is there more?"

"I'm done."

"Are you sure?"

She nodded.

"Well, if that's all you have, then you don't have enough to scare me away," he said.

She hugged him.

"What would it take? To scare you away—"

Teffinger thought about it and said, "A cupboard with no coffee in it."

88

Day Ten—July 21
Wednesday

The looters hadn't fallen for the coin trap, at least not yet, meaning they were still out there somewhere. Amaury came to Paris and moved in with Deja, ostensibly to protect her, at least until the word got out that the Egyptian government had possession of the treasure. Wednesday morning, Alexandra called Deja at the law firm and asked if she could meet for lunch.

Deja was swamped but could break away for a quick one.

"Bring Amaury," she said.

"I'm already planning on it."

At lunch, Deja had something interesting to report. "Yves Petit did a lot of legal work for Nicholas Ringer. Yves sat down to close up loose ends on some of the open files he was working on, since Ringer's now dead. It turned out that Ringer fabricated the purchase and sale of a yacht a couple of weeks ago at Yves' office. The purchasers didn't really exist. They were actors and the certified check they gave as a down payment had actually been bankrolled by Ringer."

"Why would he do that?" Alexandra asked.

"As far as I can figure, it was a convoluted way for him to meet me," Deja said. "That day, we got to talking about Remy, who had been killed a week earlier. Ringer nonchalantly offered to hire a P.I. to help find Remy's killer. His motive, in my opinion, was to get close to me. That way, if you got squirrelly and started doing something you shouldn't, Ringer would find out about it through me. He was setting himself up as his own spy, in effect."

"Sneaky."

"Very."

"I got a call this morning from Cairo," Alexandra said.

She paused and said nothing else.

"And?" Deja asked.

"And, it was a pretty interesting call."

Deja rolled her eyes.

"Come on, girl, spit it out."

"Okay, it goes like this," Alexandra said. "First of all, the credit for finding the treasure is going to go to me, you, my parents and your uncle, Remy. But that's not the big news."

"That's pretty big to me," Deja said.

Well, true.

Actually it was but there was more, much more.

"Okay, what I'm about to tell you is completely off limits to ever repeat," Alexandra said. "There are only a handful of people in the world who know what I'm about to say."

Really?

Yes.

She was serious.

Dead serious.

"So spit it out," Deja said.

"Okay, here goes," Alexandra said. "One of the jars in the cave turned out to be filled with documents, apparently authored by the rich guy who masterminded the robbery in the first place. In those notes, he talks about a pharaoh who ruled about 1500 B.C. He was an incredibly important person in his time and ruled for more than twenty years, meaning he had accumulated a considerable wealth. His tomb has never been found, to this day. The notes talk about his tomb. They describe it as being located in a southern area. Where we were was west of the Valley of the Kings, where most of the tombs have been found. South of that, in an area we never went to, is a place called the Valley of the Queens. That's where Cleopatra was buried, plus many more. The location of this new tomb is south of the Valley of the Queens. That's an area no one has really explored."

"Interesting," Deja said.

"No, that's not interesting," Alexandra said. "Here's what's interesting. They want me to head up the expedition to find it."

"Wow," Deja said. "Congratulations."

Alexandra leaned across the table and whispered into Deja's ear, "And I want you and Amaury to join me."

Before Deja could react, Amaury leaned over and whispered into her other ear, "I already said yes."

Deja must have had a deer-in-headlights look because they both laughed.

Then Alexandra slid an airplane ticket across the table. "If you're ready to make history—make that more history—we leave on Friday. Don't worry about money. We'll have tons of it. More than you'd ever make being a lawyer."

Deja retreated in thought and put a worried look on her face.

"Are there snakes in that area?"

Alexandra shrugged.

"Yeah, probably."

Deja stuffed the ticket in her back pocket.

"Good, I'm kind of missing the little fellows."

89

Day Twelve—July 23
Friday

Teffinger and Fallon worked the caveman case Wednesday, Thursday and Friday before officially resigning themselves to defeat. Whoever gouged out Amanda Peterson's eyes in Denver would forever be a mystery.

It was over.

The man had won.

Painful as it was, that was the end result.

Sometimes that happened.

The best thing to do was just accept it.

Let it go.

Move on.

They did, however, find out a couple of interesting things over the last few days. According to files found in the house of Marcel Durand, he had actually been contacted by Emmanuelle at Blue Moon to find out who killed Sharla DePaglia.

Teffinger chuckled.

"Can you imagine the look on his face when she gave him

the assignment," he said. "That's probably the first time in history where a P.I. killed someone and then got the job to investigate it—to find himself, in effect."

"I wonder what he was going to do," Fallon said. "Other than take the money and pretend he was working the case."

"He had to give up someone's name eventually," Teffinger said. "That's the only way he could get Emmanuelle to close the file. He'd probably give her the name of someone he didn't like and kill two birds with one Blue Moon."

She nodded.

Yeah, that's what he'd do.

That's exactly what he'd do.

Files found on Nicholas Ringer's yacht in Nice also provided an interesting story. It turned out that Ringer hired Durand to run down a license plate number that Durand then traced to Luc Trickett.

They didn't know why.

Not for two days.

Then Fallon said, "This is speculation, but here's what I think happened. Nicholas Ringer went to the house to kidnap Michelle Berri. His girlfriend, Nodja Lefebvre, was waiting down the street, keeping a lookout. She saw someone leave the house just after Ringer went in. She wrote down his license plate number."

Teffinger cocked his head.

Interesting.

Go on.

"Ringer goes inside and finds Tracy White dead. He doesn't freak, though. He waits until Michelle Berri comes home and then abducts her as planned. Later, Nodja tells him just how close he came to whoever it was that was in the house just before him, meaning the person who killed Tracy White. Now Ringer starts to wonder if the man saw him."

"Thinking he was a possible witness," Teffinger said.

Exactly.

"Two ships crossing in the night," Teffinger added. "Crossing a little too close."

Precisely.

"So he hired Durand to find out who was driving the car. Durand traced it to Luc Trickett," Fallon said. "Then Ringer had Durand kill Trickett, just so there wouldn't be any loose ends. Unfortunately for Durand, a neighbor saw him leaving the house."

"Very impressive," Teffinger said.

"That means Trickett is the one who gouged out Tracy White's eyes," she said.

Why?

Why?

Why?

He wasn't a caveman, he was a boxer.

Teffinger had a flight scheduled out of CDG back to Denver at 9:18 p.m. tonight. Tomorrow, he'd go to the office, tie up loose ends, and officially hand his resignation to Double-F Tanker, the chief.

Tanker would scream and kick and moan but Teffinger would be ready for him.

Sydney would cry.

Katie Baxter would swear.

And Paul Kwak would remind him that there aren't any cool cars in France.

He wouldn't be ready for any of that but he'd have to handle it, somehow.

Then he'd meet with a realtor and get his house on the market.

On Tuesday or Wednesday, he'd fly back to Paris.

Fallon was going to take two weeks off.

They'd spend most of it in the museums.

With Renoir.

Van Gogh.

Degas.

And other people Teffinger didn't even know yet.

Friday evening, Fallon dropped Teffinger off at the airport, kissed him goodbye and said, "See you next week." Then she headed back to the houseboat.

Clouds rolled in and the wind kicked up.

The Seine got choppy.

The boat rocked.

She drank wine, watched TV, read a magazine and went to bed.

90

Fallon was sound asleep when her head exploded into colors. She knew she'd been hit with something and opened her eyes just long enough to see the dark silhouette of a man above her. Before she could scream, something hit her again even harder and everything went black. She woke up at some point later, which could have been two minutes or three hours.

She tried to move but couldn't.

She was tied spread-eagle on the bed.

Naked.

She pulled wildly but it did no good.

She could barely budge.

She was stretched tight.

Immobile.

She tried to scream but couldn't.

She was gagged.

Outside the wind howled with a terrible, demon fierceness.

Lightning crackled.

Rain pummeled against the windows.

Suddenly the black shape of a man appeared above her. He straddled her stomach, tweaked her nipples and said, "You're awake. Good."

She recognized the voice but couldn't place it.

The man set a knife on her chest between her breasts.

"I've been wanting to do this ever since that first day in your office," he said. "Ever since the first time I saw them—and by them, I'm referring to your eyes, of course. There are certain eyes that just need to be turned around and pointed the other way."

Suddenly she knew where she'd heard the voice before.

It belonged to that lawyer, the caveman lawyer.

Paul Sabater.

The one who came to her office and accounted for his whereabouts at the time Tracy White was killed.

"You're probably wondering if I cut out the eyes before or after I kill the person," he said. "So far, it's always been after. But this time, I'm going to change things around a little bit. This time I'm going to do it before."

Lightning exploded, followed by a terrible crack of thunder.

"You deserve one last meal, so to speak, before you depart on your final journey," he said. "So I'm going to give it to you, in the form of a story, to quench that thirsty little detective's mind of yours. That's fair, don't you think?"

He picked up the knife and ran the tip across her forehead, around her eyes and over the bridge of her nose.

Then he set it back down on her chest.

"I'm the one who killed Amanda Peterson in Denver," he said. "But she wasn't the first. She wasn't even in the top five. I've had lots of trips over the years—Tokyo, Bangkok, Australia, just to name a few. I always leave my signature mark behind, so to speak."

He ran a finger softly on her nipple.

"In Denver, someone saw me in the stairwell after I killed Amanda Peterson," he said. "She cooperated with the cops. That really pissed me off. Her name was Tracy White. I hung around to kill her but failed—one of the few times in my life, I might add. Then one day something weird happened. I saw her in La Defense. Of course, she had to die, not just because I still wanted her dead, but because sooner or later she'd bump into me and end up calling the cops. So she was a threat."

Lightning exploded.

The room lit, just for a heartbeat but long enough for Fallon to see the look on the man's face.

It was the look on an animal, an animal about to devour its prey.

She tugged at her bonds.

He smiled.

"That's a nice touch," he said. "Thank you for that."

"Anyway, to continue with your last meal, I'm a lawyer, which you already know," he said. "That means I'm smarter than the average bear. Instead of killing Tracy White myself—as much as I wanted to—I decided to hire someone to do it. The man I hired was a lowlife named Luc Trickett. His instructions were to gouge out her eyes and turn them around, just like I would have done." He smiled. "I know what you're thinking. Why didn't I just have Trickett slit her throat? Why have him gouge out her eyes?"

He studied her.

"The answer's easy," he said. "Nick Teffinger pissed me off as much as Tracy White did, even more. I wanted him to suffer. Having him think that Amanda Peterson's killer got Tracy White would do just that, since he was the one who gave away her name. Anyway, Trickett had no problem with the eyes-gouging part of it. I went to Madrid and made sure I had a rock-solid alibi at the time."

He sighed.

"Afterwards, of course, I killed Trickett and cleaned out his files," he said. "It's called the no-witnesses theory. I shot him three times in the head. I enjoyed it. The world is a better place with him gone."

A fierce gust of wind rocked the boat.

"It's getting nasty out there." He grinned and added, "Not as nasty as in here, but still—"

He picked up the knife and passed it back and forth between his hands in front of her face.

A taste.

"It's incredibly sharp," he said. "Razor sharp. You probably won't feel a thing. Then again, you might. It's hard to say."

He paused as if gathering his thoughts.

"The thing that threw me is when that sketch appeared on page 5 of the newspaper," he said. "Since I had nothing to do with Tracy White, I knew it had to be a re-draw of the Denver sketch. That was a stroke of genius, by the way, very clever. I was impressed and still am. But it also presented a problem. There was a danger someone might think it was me and call my name in. I didn't know what would happen at that point. I was afraid that you would check to see if I was in Denver when Amanda Peterson got killed. If you had, you would have found out quite easily that I was. That would have raised your eyebrows, at the very least, and you would have dug deeper. So I decided to cut your investigation off at the knees, before it even began. I came to your office, voluntarily, and gave you all the information on my rock-solid alibi for the time Tracy White got killed, hoping you'd see me as a dead end." He sighed. "Unfortunately for you, you did."

He ran a finger across her lips.

"Luc Trickett, by the way, didn't have anything to do with Tracy White's roommate, Michelle Berri," he said. "She wasn't there when he killed Tracy. She must have come home afterwards and got taken by someone else for some other reason. That part of it is still a mystery to me, but one that I don't care too much about, if you want to know the truth."

Lightning flashed.

Then again.

Thunder rolled over Paris.

"Enough chitchat," he said. "Your last meal has now been fully served. I've done my job and now it's time for you to do yours."

He picked up the knife and positioned the tip just below her eye.

"Are you ready?"

91

Day Twelve—July 23
Friday Night

————————

Suddenly the man gurgled and fell to the side. A flash of lightning showed a knife sticking out the back of his head as he dropped to the floor.

Another man was in the room.

Teffinger.

He untied her.

Then he held her tight and rocked her.

She cried.

The storm beat down.

After a long time she asked, "Why aren't you on a plane?"

"My flight didn't officially get cancelled, but it got delayed because of the storm, and then I got too scared to fly," Teffinger said. "So I came back until tomorrow. I hope you don't mind."

She exhaled.

"Too scared to fly? You're such a baby sometimes."

"I was hoping you wouldn't notice."

About the Author

Formerly a longstanding trial attorney before taking the big leap and devoting his fulltime attention to writing, RJ Jagger (that's a penname, by the way) is the author of over twenty hard-edged mystery and suspense thrillers. In addition to his own books, Jagger also ghostwrites for a well-known, bestselling author. He a member of both the International Thriller Writers and the Mystery Writers of America..

RJJAGGER.com